'You mea... 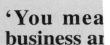 ...business ar...

He could tell b... ...tone of her voice that the idea appealed to her. Steven shrugged. 'We don't need to write the terms down in stone, do we? You need a partner at this wedding. I've got a few engagements when I need a woman by my side.'

'And it would be just a straightforward arrangement that would suit us both,' she reiterated.

'Why do you keep emphasising that?' Steven asked tersely. 'Because I'm not your type?'

'Maybe I'm not your type either, Steven,' she said quietly. 'That can work two ways.'

But the truth of the matter was that Chloe was starting to think that he was very much her type. Maybe that was why she was so keen to emphasise the fact just now that anything between them would be strictly business…she was desperately trying to keep her feet on the ground where he was concerned. Desperately trying not to think about how much she wanted to kiss him again, because she knew he spelt danger.

Kathryn Ross was born in Zambia, where her parents happened to live at that time. Educated in Ireland and England, she now lives in a village near Blackpool, Lancashire. Kathryn is a professional beauty therapist, but writing is her first love. As a child she wrote adventure stories, and at thirteen was editor of her school magazine. Happily, ten writing years later, DESIGNED WITH LOVE was accepted by Mills & Boon®. A romantic Sagittarian, she loves travelling to exotic locations.

Recent titles by the same author:

THE ELEVENTH-HOUR GROOM
THE NIGHT OF THE WEDDING
HER DETERMINED HUSBAND

THE MILLIONAIRE'S AGENDA

BY
KATHRYN ROSS

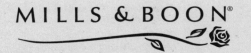
MILLS & BOON®

First published in Great Britain 2002
Harlequin Mills & Boon Limited,
Eton House, 18-24 Paradise Road, Richmond, Surrey TW9 1SR

© Kathryn Ross 2002

ISBN 0 263 82941 3

Set in Times Roman 10½ on 11½ pt.
01-0602-50956

Printed and bound in Spain
by Litografía Rosés, S.A., Barcelona

CHAPTER ONE

CHLOE glanced up from her typing and her eyes fell on the calendar on her desk. It was three weeks until her half-sister's wedding! She could feel a wave of panic creeping over her as she thought about attending on her own. Then she was angry with herself. It was no big deal; lots of women attended social gatherings alone these days, she told herself firmly. She wasn't going to feel pressurised about it.

She turned her attention to the last of the letters on her desk and flicked a glance at her wrist-watch; it was four-thirty, almost time to go home. Usually at this time on a Friday evening she would have felt happy, the weekend would have stretched before her, filled with glorious free-dom. Nile might have taken her to dinner or to a new wine bar or...

She switched her mind away from Nile. The engagement was off; Nile was a thing of the past. At the age of twenty-nine, she was once again single. Two years wasted on a man who had turned from Prince Charming into Quasimodo in one afternoon. How could she have been so stupid? she asked herself for what had to be the hundredth time.

The printer next to her spewed out the letters and she snapped them up, running an eye over them to check for any errors, trying very hard not to think about Nile Flynn for one moment longer. Trouble was, it was very difficult, especially as she was in a complete financial mess because of him.

The connecting door through to the inner sanctum of the

office opened and Steven Cavendish's voice boomed out. 'Chloe, did you ring Manchester to inform them I'd be up there tomorrow?'

'Yes, Steven, I did.'

'What about Mr Steel—did you deal with that problem in the Waterside Restaurant?'

'Yes, it's all sorted out.' Chloe stood up and ran a smoothing hand down over her smart black suit, mentally preparing herself to face Steven Cavendish. She needed to ask him for a pay rise, had been waiting all week for the right moment to bring the subject up, but unfortunately there didn't seem to be a right time to catch her boss these days.

He had been involved in months of lengthy negotiations to secure a takeover bid of a chain of restaurants and the strain of long hours plus a series of setbacks had made him unusually grouchy. But she really couldn't wait any longer, she told herself firmly. Whether it was the right moment or not she was going to have to ask him tonight before leaving.

Chloe reached for the desk diary, picked up the letters that she needed him to sign and with a determined stride headed into the heart of the Cavendish kingdom.

She was momentarily taken aback to find that her boss wasn't seated behind his enormous desk, but was standing with his back to the office, looking out at the wintry silver cast of the London skyline.

'Weather forecast says it's going to snow,' she said briskly. 'You'd better allow extra travelling time for your journey up north tomorrow.'

'Yes…thanks, Chloe, but I don't think a bit of snow will affect the company jet.'

'Actually they are predicting blizzard conditions.'

'Are they? Well, as they rarely get their predictions right, I'll worry about that tomorrow.'

'Please yourself.' Chloe put the letters down on the desk. 'You need to sign these…oh, and John Hunt asked if you would ring him back before six.'

Steven didn't turn from his contemplation of the outside world.

She noticed he had taken the jacket of his suit off; it was hung over the back of his chair.

Chloe's eyes flicked over his tall, broad-shouldered frame. For a man who spent long hours stuck behind a desk he had a very attractive body, powerfully honed and very masculine.

The first time she had met him when she had come here for an interview two years ago she had been quite bowled over by just how attractive Steven Cavendish was. Raven-dark hair and dark eyes that seemed to slice straight into her very soul had unnerved her slightly. He had the cool confidence of a person very much at ease with himself, very aware of his own powerful sensuality. He was also a complete stickler to work for and that, oddly enough, had been a wonderful salvation for their working relationship.

Chloe liked his straightforward businesslike approach. She enjoyed the challenges that working for him presented, maybe because she was a bit of a perfectionist herself. After the first week she had forgotten to be overwhelmed by his good looks, and anyway she'd had Nile in her life. Besides which there really hadn't been time for such matters in the fast pace of their office. She'd had to focus solidly on her job as his PA. And, though she said it herself, they made a formidable team.

She tore her eyes away from Steven and opened her diary. 'Renaldo rang to say he's running late, but he'll be here for your appointment around five-thirty.'

'Great—another late evening.' Steven's voice was dry.

'Oh, and I ordered the bouquet of flowers to be delivered

to your house on Wednesday afternoon. A dozen red roses, as you requested.'

'Thanks.'

He must be going to deliver the roses in person, she thought. Chloe wondered fleetingly about this latest development between him and his glamorous girlfriend Helen. She had organised many a bouquet for his women over the last two years but never red roses. Then again, according to the grapevine in the office, none of the women he had dated since the death of his wife three years ago seemed to have lasted as long as Helen Smyth-Jones.

Chloe tapped her pencil against the diary as she waited for him to spring into action. After two years she knew her boss fairly well, had learnt to judge all his moods so that she could evaluate pretty accurately what was coming next.

She knew now, for instance, not to be misled by this quiet, reflective stance. When Steven Cavendish fell silent he was usually at his most dangerous, the quicksilver of his mind regrouping, planning ahead and about to burst forward with some earth-shattering remark or whirlwind of activity.

She flicked over the pages of the diary as she waited for him. It was best to adopt a laid-back attitude when Steven was like this. To try and hurry him into signing the letters, or indeed to try and swing the conversation towards her pay rise, would be a big mistake at the moment.

'It's Beth's sixth birthday next week, isn't it?' she reflected softly. It was an observation, not a reminder. Chloe spent her time reminding Steven about appointments and schedules but she didn't have to remind him about his daughter. Beth was the one person who took priority in his mind over business.

'Yes, it is. You remember everything, don't you?' Steven turned around then and looked at her, his dark eyes skimming sketchily over the glasses she always wore and the way her honey-blonde hair was severely drawn back from her face. Chloe was used to him looking at her like that, as if he was seeing her but focusing on something else.

'Well...I write everything down. And it's my job to remember everything,' she said quietly.

He nodded. 'Well, we can't stand about talking all day,' he muttered. 'Better get these letters signed.'

Chloe smiled to herself. She had been right; Steven was focused on something else, and as usual it was work.

'Did you ask John Hunt what he wanted to talk to me about?'

'Yes, it's the normal problems at the Cavendish Cuisine Restaurant,' Chloe answered. 'He said to tell you that the chef there may be a creative genius, but he's as mad as the proverbial March hare.'

Steven grunted and pulled out his chair to sit back behind his desk. 'John is the damn manager there; I pay him to take care of those problems. Send him an e-mail and tell him I said to just deal with it.' There was a steely note in the firm voice. Steven Cavendish wouldn't tolerate anyone who couldn't pull his or her weight. Chloe didn't rate John's chances of lasting long within the company if he didn't start showing some initiative. The boss was not renowned for being sentimental when it came to weeding out any dead wood from the company. In fact, there were times that Chloe thought Steven could be quite ruthless, but then, she supposed you didn't get to be a self-made millionaire by the age of thirty-eight unless you could play hard-ball.

Steven finished signing the last letter and then pushed them across the desk towards her. 'Is everything set for the board meeting next week?'

'Yes, and I ordered some refreshments from the Galley Restaurant. Just sandwiches and a few assorted cakes from the continental selection in their bakery.'

'What, not baking them yourself?' Steven looked up, a

glimmer of teasing humour lighting his dark gaze for just a moment.

'Give me Monday morning off and I'll see what I can do,' she retorted swiftly.

He laughed. '*Touché*. Sorry, Chloe, didn't mean to sound patronising. It's just that you never cease to amaze me; you are always so clued up, so in front with everything.'

This was it, her opportunity to ask for her increase in salary, and she jumped in quickly before the moment was lost. 'I'm glad that you're pleased with my work, Steven. But if you have a few moments there is something I'd like to discuss.'

'Fire away.' Steven put down his pen and waved her towards the chair opposite. 'What's the problem?'

'No problem as such,' she said brightly, and tried not to think about the massive demands for immediate payment that lay on her desk at home.

'Good. Things have been pretty hectic around here, haven't they? It's unfortunate timing with you planning a wedding soon.' As he spoke Steven was riffling through some papers on his desk, looking for something. 'How's that going, anyway?' he asked absently. 'Are you any nearer finalising the purchase of your new house?'

'Well, we've paid the deposit…' Chloe felt herself tensing up. She wasn't surprised that Steven hadn't noticed she was no longer wearing her engagement ring. She supposed she should say something…tell him the relationship was finished, that the purchase of her new house would not be going through…but they only ever discussed their personal life in passing, and even then in the most offhand way.

She couldn't just tell Steven that her fiancé had run off and left her with a load of bills for a wedding that would now never take place, plus he had emptied their joint bank account. All Steven was concerned about in relation to her was her work, and that was fine by her.

Now, for instance, he had asked her questions, but he wasn't waiting for her reply—he was more interested in looking for something on his desk.

'What are you searching for?' she asked him as he flicked through the papers again.

'The notes from that last meeting with Renaldo,' he muttered. 'You haven't seen them, have you?'

'Blue folder underneath,' she told him and watched as he went straight to the relevant papers.

'Thanks, Chloe.' He smiled at her. 'Now, where were we?'

'Well, I—'

The phone rang on his desk and with a brief apology he snatched it up. 'Steven Cavendish,' he said briskly.

Chloe sat back in her seat and tried to relax. It was always like this in here; there was rarely a space to breathe, let alone talk.

She wondered why she felt so incredibly tense.

The worst that could happen was that Steven would say no to the pay rise, and if he did she had an alternative option. The company she had worked for previously two years ago had recently contacted her and asked her to come back, had offered a ten per cent increase on whatever Cavendish were paying.

Trouble was, she didn't really want to go back there. She liked working for Cavendish. She felt her career was going places here; it was much more go-ahead. The money was pretty good here as well; if it weren't for this damn situation with her finances she would be quite content to leave the status quo.

Her eyes rested on Steven's face. 'I need a little more information before I answer that,' he said. 'OK, well, just get the figures and I'll look up the report; phone me back.'

'Who was that?' Chloe asked automatically as he put the receiver down.

'Nothing—just the accounts department; they want some clarification on one of the Renaldo restaurants in Paris.'

'They will want the list I printed out yesterday; it's in my desk.'

'Well, it will do later.' Steven leaned back in his chair and glanced at his watch. 'Renaldo doesn't want to come in until five-thirty anyway.'

'Yes. So, as I was saying, Steven—' Chloe pressed on swiftly, but once again the phone rang.

Maybe she should send him a letter, Chloe thought wryly. Or go back out into her office and phone through on the extension. It seemed the only way she was going to get an undivided minute of his time.

She sat watching him, thinking it was probably the accounts department again, and started to feel impatient. Maybe she should just hand in her notice and take the offer from her old company? At least back at Brittas there had been time to speak to her boss occasionally.

Then she saw Steven's face blanch. 'Gina, calm down.' His voice was crisp and authoritarian. 'I can't work out what you are saying. Is Beth all right?'

Chloe leaned forward in concern, her exasperation forgotten as she realised something was very wrong.

'OK.' Steven glanced at his watch. 'I'll be home directly.'

The phone slammed down, Steven got to his feet and reached for his jacket. 'I'm sorry, Chloe, but whatever you wanted to say will have to wait until later. I've got to go home. That was my childminder, Gina.'

'Is Beth all right?' she asked anxiously.

'Yes…it's Gina's father. He's been taken to hospital and she has to leave.'

'But you've got another appointment with the director of Renaldo,' Chloe said, aghast. 'He said it was urgent.'

'You'll just have to apologise for me,' Steven muttered.

'I've no one to watch Beth. My mother is on holiday and—'

'I'll go,' Chloe said impulsively.

Steven stopped in the process of opening one of the drawers to get his car keys. 'You?'

'I'm quite capable of watching a five-year-old,' she murmured crossly. 'And this meeting with Renaldo is important. It might just be the turning point you've been waiting for with this takeover bid.'

Steven's eyes narrowed on her thoughtfully. As always her clear, confident tones dispelled any theory that lurking behind those scholarly glasses was a shy librarian-type.

'It makes sense for me to go, don't you think?' she persisted when he didn't answer her immediately.

'Yes, I suppose it does. Did you drive to work today?'

She nodded. 'My car is downstairs.'

He put his keys back in the drawer and closed it. 'Thanks, Chloe, I really appreciate this. I'll try not to be too long here, so I don't take up the whole of your Friday evening.'

'I wasn't doing anything tonight anyway,' Chloe said as she got up.

Steven watched her from the doorway as she quickly organised herself and then left. Then he sat back down behind his desk.

That phone call had rattled him. In the few garbled seconds as he'd tried to make out what Gina was saying he had instantly feared that something was wrong with Beth. And the memories of another call, the moment when he had known he'd lost his wife, had immediately flooded back. Maybe the recollection had been so vivid because it was coming up to the anniversary of Stephanie's death and he had been thinking about her earlier this afternoon. It was almost three years ago to the day. Where had that time gone? What had he done with it? He felt as if he had been wandering around in a blinkered haze through most of it.

From nowhere he remembered his mother telling him in that sensible, no-nonsense tone of hers that he needed to find a wife and a mother for Beth. He had answered in an equally firm tone, telling her that he didn't need a wife. But it was at times like this when he wondered if his mother was right. It was difficult being a single parent and running a big business. And he desperately wanted Beth to be secure and happy.

Steven shook his head, impatient with himself for worrying like this. Beth had a secure environment. Their lives ran smoothly. Gina was great with Beth and he had capable Chloe winging her way there now.

But if he did decide he wanted to settle down and get married again, there was Helen.

The notion crept surreptitiously from the back of his mind, where it had been simmering for a while. He was well aware that their relationship had come to a crossroads. She wanted more from him and he was hesitating. Steven couldn't figure out why he was. Helen was beautiful and bright and, although she hadn't been entirely relaxed around Beth at first, that was only to be expected...wasn't it? She had never been married before, never had children, and she was a very high-powered career woman.

Anyway, she was a lot better around Beth these days...he told himself forcefully...a lot more at ease. But even as he said the words to himself he knew deep down that what he had with Helen wasn't really enough...not for marriage.

The phone rang again and swiftly he picked it up. It was the accounts department again. Remembering that Chloe had said the information they needed was in her desk, he put them on hold and went through to her office.

He smiled to himself as he noticed how tidy and organised her desk was. To one side were lists of the day's appointments, along with specific notes of reference so that she could brief him fully before each.

He slid open the top drawer; it contained blank stationery, and he was going to close it again when he noticed a letter tucked to one side. The printed heading was a company name he vaguely recognised. Curiously he took it out and read it.

It was from the managing director Chloe used to work for. He skimmed through it with a rising feeling of horror. They had recently expanded and were headhunting her, offering an increase on whatever Cavendish were paying!

Steven sat down in her chair and stared at the letter. Was this what she had wanted to talk to him about this afternoon? Had she been about to hand in her notice? He was stunned and then appalled as the full realisation of how much of a gap Chloe's leaving would make.

She couldn't go—it was unthinkable!

CHAPTER TWO

THE clouds seemed unusually low in the sky; there was a strange yellow cast to them that reflected off the roads, giving London a sepia glow. A smoky shroud hung over the Houses of Parliament and swirled over the river Thames, and in amongst this eerie setting there was the usual chaotic, very modern Friday-night scramble for people to get home.

Usually Chloe would be amongst the crush of people heading down into the underground. Her flat was central and she didn't generally bother with her car because of this traffic. Today, however, she had wanted the solitude of her own vehicle, which was just as well, she thought now as she switched on her radio to catch the traffic reports. Steven couldn't have risked not meeting with Renaldo.

It seemed to take for ever before Chloe was out of the jams and heading south. She wondered if Steven ever got fed up with this long business of commuting every day. Then she turned her car into the picturesque village of Hemsworth, with its thatched cottages and village green, and remembered why he might think this journey was worth it.

As she turned into Steven's driveway the light was fading fast and the first flurry of snow started to hit the windscreen. The ivy-clad Georgian manor was a welcome sight, its mullioned windows alight with welcoming warmth.

She pulled the car to a halt and hurried up to the front door, battling against the sudden gust of a bitter breeze that blew snow into her eyes and mouth. She lifted her hand towards the heavy knocker on the red front door but it swung open before she could use it.

'Thank heavens you're here.' Gina was already dressed in a heavy coat; she was pulling on gloves and a woollen hat over her thick dark hair as she spoke.

'I got here as quickly as I could.' Chloe stepped into the warmth of the house.

'I know; Steven phoned me and told me how long you'd be,' the girl murmured tearfully. 'Thanks for coming, Chloe. I'm just so worried about Dad.'

'I hope he's OK.'

Gina nodded and hurried out of the door. 'Try and phone Steven tomorrow some time; let him know how things are,' Chloe called after her as she ran across the driveway towards her car.

Gina waved, but whatever she called back was lost in the wind.

Chloe turned her attention back into the house. Beth stood further down the hallway. She looked like a little lost soul: her long blonde curls were rumpled, as if she had been standing on her head, and she was wearing a pair of dungarees and a pink jumper and only one shoe on her foot; the other dangled in her hand as if she been in the process of trying to put it on. Chloe got the distinct impression that she had wanted to go with Gina.

'Hello, Beth.' Chloe grinned at her, putting a determinedly cheerful tone in her voice as she pushed the door closed behind her. 'My goodness, but it's cold outside. I'm glad I'm here with you in this nice warm house.'

'Is Daddy coming home soon?' The bright blue eyes gazed up at her solemnly.

'Yes, Daddy will be home very soon.' Chloe took off her coat and hung it up. 'He's just got one more meeting. Meanwhile, I'm going to look after you.'

Beth made no reply to that. Chloe crouched down so that

she was on eye level with the little girl. 'Have you had your supper yet?'

Beth shook her head. 'Gina was going to make sausage and chips.'

'That sounds great. Shall I make that for us?'

'If you want.'

'Come on, then. You lead the way to the kitchen.'

Beth was very quiet, Chloe thought as they walked down the hallway. She wondered if she was just feeling shy. Although Beth had met her on several occasions when she'd had to come out to the house on business, the little girl didn't know her that well.

Chloe had never been in Steven's kitchen before. It was enormous, with a huge refectory table at one end and so many cupboards that it took ages to find something as simple as a cup. She remembered Steven telling her that this house had once been the old vicarage, and a path led directly through the gardens to the picturesque church of St Mary. It wasn't hard to imagine the vicar's wife in here, baking scones for the village fête. The house had a lovely, homely atmosphere.

'Gina was crying before you came,' Beth said as she watched her filling the kettle and opening and closing doors.

'That's because she's worried about her dad.'

Beth sat on one of the chairs at the table. 'Will Gina's daddy die?' she asked suddenly, and her voice wobbled precariously.

Chloe looked over at her, and suddenly she knew why she was quieter than usual; she wasn't shy, she was worried. 'He's very poorly, but people get sick and then they get better again when they take the right medicine.'

'Or they go to heaven like Mummy.' Beth kicked her foot against the leg of the table. 'I don't want my daddy to be sick and go to hospital.'

Chloe went across to her and knelt down beside her. 'Your daddy is fine, Beth,' she said gently. 'He's back at the office working really hard.'

'He hasn't gone to hospital?'

'No, darling, he's his usual self. A bit grouchy now and then, but on the whole wonderful.'

Beth giggled at that, and looked a lot happier.

Smiling, Chloe went back to making the dinner. 'You know, you remind me of someone in a nursery rhyme,' she said. 'Someone with one shoe on and one shoe off—was it Humpty Dumpty?'

Beth thought about this for a moment then shook her head.

'Was it the three blind mice?'

Beth giggled. 'Mice don't wear shoes, silly.'

It was strange how the sound of a child's laughter was so infectious. Chloe found herself smiling as she worked. And it was only later, after they had eaten and she was clearing away the dishes, that she realised that for the first time in weeks she had gone several hours without thinking once about Nile.

Steven closed the front door with a feeling of relief. What a night, he thought, shaking the snow off his coat before hanging it up in the vestibule.

'Hello?' He walked down the hallway, expecting to find Chloe in the lounge. He was impatient to talk to her about this business of her leaving. But all the lights were off in the lounge and the fire was dwindling down to just a red glow.

He retraced his steps and went upstairs.

The bedside lamp was still on in Beth's room and it cast a warm pink light over the patchwork quilt and the peacefully sleeping child. Steven went over to tuck her in and kiss her cheek. Then his eyes moved to Chloe, who was curled up in the chair next to her. She was also fast asleep.

He wondered suddenly if he had been working her too hard recently. Perhaps he was even a little bit guilty of taking her for granted? That would change if he could persuade her to stay, he told himself.

His eyes moved over her. She looked vulnerable in sleep; her glasses were pushed up on top of her head, and she looked different without them. Steven noticed the delicate heart-shape of her face, and the fact that her cheekbones were well-defined. Her dark lashes looked incredibly long against the pallor of her skin. Her mouth curved in a soft smile. She was exceptionally pretty—why had he never noticed that before?

He smiled as he noted Beth's storybook balancing from her fingertips, about to drop at any moment to the floor. But as he took the book from her he frowned as he noticed for the first time that she was no longer wearing her engagement ring. How long had that been missing?

Now he came to think about it, she hadn't been her usual bouncy self these last few weeks. Her customary cheerful optimism that usually made him smile had been completely absent.

'Chloe?' He touched her arm gently, feeling almost protective about her; she looked so young and vulnerable sleeping there. 'Chloe, honey, wake up.'

Her eyes flickered open; bright sapphire-blue, they stared up at him and for a moment he felt as disorientated as she looked. She had the most gorgeous eyes...why had he never noticed that before either?

'Nile...?' She murmured the name huskily.

'No, it's Steven. You're at my house, remember?'

'Oh...yes.' If there was a faint flicker of disappointment in her eyes her lashes came down swiftly to hide her emotions. 'I'm sorry, I don't usually doze off like that. I guess

I must be making up for the fact that I've had some sleepless nights recently.'

He watched as she tried to gather herself together, smoothing down her skirt, slipping her feet back into her shoes and then running her fingers over the arms of the chair as she searched for her glasses.

'Have you seen my glasses anywhere?' she murmured, looking around her in an unfocused way.

He reached out and pulled them down from the top of her head, smiling as he noticed the bright flush of embarrassment in her cheeks.

'Sorry…I haven't woken up yet.'

'Stop apologising. I should be apologising to you for keeping you here so late.' He sat on the edge of the bed, his knees almost touching hers. 'Thanks for coming over here, Chloe.'

'That's OK. I don't mind at all.'

Unless it was her imagination, Steven seemed to be looking at her very intently, most unlike the way he usually looked at her. She felt such a mess. She tried to push her hair back neatly into place as tendrils escaped to curl softly around her face. 'What time is it?'

He glanced at his gold wrist-watch. 'Almost ten o'clock.'

Steven glanced back up at her and something about the way his dark eyes moved over her face made her stomach dip.

Maybe it was his close proximity but Chloe felt suddenly very conscious of him, very aware of the raw power of his masculinity.

He smiled. 'Come on downstairs and we'll have a drink.'

'No, I'd better go.' She stood up. 'I've got loads to do at home and I want to have a shower.'

'Chloe, you can't go anywhere tonight,' Steven told her softly. 'The weather is diabolical, and so are the roads. It's taken me ages to get home. You're welcome to stay in the spare bedroom.'

'It can't be that bad, surely?' She crossed over to look out of the bedroom window. The snow was coming down so heavily that it almost obliterated the driveway in a white-out.

'Dire, isn't it?' Steven said. 'You'd never think it was April.'

'No, you wouldn't.' Chloe pulled the curtains closed and turned to look at him. 'Guess you're stuck with me, then.'

'Well, I'm hoping so.'

The tone of his voice seemed strangely weighted on those words and he was watching her with an intensity that she really wasn't used to.

'Chloe, you are not thinking of handing in your notice at work, are you?'

The abrupt question took her aback. 'Why are you asking me that?'

'I was looking for the list for the accounts department and I found that letter from Brittas in your desk,' he said quietly.

'Oh…I see.' She felt her skin colouring with embarrassment as she remembered leaving the letter there in order to answer it in her lunch hour, but lunch had been overtaken by work and she hadn't got around to it. 'I was going to talk to you about that this afternoon—'

'So are you thinking of leaving?' Steven stood up from the bed. 'Look, whatever Brittas are offering I'll better,' he said sharply.

The intensity of his tone startled her. 'Well, actually, I wasn't going to hand in my notice. I was going to ask you for a pay rise,' she said truthfully.

'Really?' He pushed a hand through the darkness of his hair. 'Thank God for that; you gave me quite a jolt.'

'Did I?' She was quite touched by the note of sincere

relief in his voice. Then she smiled teasingly. 'Enough of a jolt to give me a pay rise?'

He laughed. 'Yes, Chloe...definitely enough for a pay rise. I'll get on to the accounts department first thing on Monday.'

'Thanks.' She smiled. 'When I was trying to get a minute of your time today to ask you this I never thought for one moment our conversation would end in Beth's bedroom.'

'No...it's been a bit of a strange day all around.'

'How did you get on with Renaldo?' she asked.

His lips slanted wryly. 'OK...I think. Renaldo is one tough cookie.'

'Did he mention the meeting with the bank last week?' She put her hand up to her hair as she felt it escaping the confines of its clips.

'Yes, he did...'

Her hair wouldn't go back in the clips, so impatiently she just let it loose, running her hand through the silky length as it tumbled around her shoulders. 'I don't suppose he brought those extra accounts with him?'

Her mind was firmly focused on the conversation, but Steven's wasn't. He was distracted by the way her hair had fallen in a long swathe around her shoulders. He noticed the golden lights amongst the darker strands of honey, giving it a rich vibrancy.

'Steven?'

'Huh?'

'Did he mention the extra accounts?'

'Yes...' Steven stared at her abstractedly. He could hardly believe how beautiful she looked with her hair down. He shook his head as he realised she was waiting for him to expand on the subject. 'Sorry, Chloe, I'm really tired. My brain seems to have gone into shut-down mode.'

'I'm not surprised; you've been in that office since eight this morning.'

'Yes, well, hopefully I'll just have a couple more weeks like this and then everything will settle down once this acquisition has gone through.'

Chloe nodded. She watched as he loosened his tie, then ran his hand over the back of his neck. 'Do you want me to make you a sandwich while you freshen up?' she asked impulsively.

He looked as if he was about to decline the offer, then he shrugged. 'Thanks, Chloe; I reckon I'm well and truly in your debt today.'

'Watch it or I might ask for another rise.' She grinned at him, a hint of mischief playing in her blue eyes now.

He watched as she moved over to check on Beth. Her fingers brushed gently to sweep a stray strand of golden curls from the child's face, and then she bent to kiss her forehead.

The gesture was completely natural and so tenderly instinctive that it startled him. Why, he couldn't have said; there was just something in the picture she presented, something familiar about the tableau of the sleeping child and the woman watching over her that jolted something inside him. Maybe it was the long golden hair that hid her face… Stephanie's hair had been long and golden, just like Chloe's.

'Was Beth good for you?' Abruptly he tried to snap out of whatever held him transfixed. He was overtired, he told himself briskly.

'Yes, she was fine.' She straightened and looked over at him. 'You're very lucky; she's a lovely child.'

'Well…I think so.' Steven shrugged. 'But then, I'm biased.' His eyes flicked to the book he had taken from her hand earlier. 'How many times did she get you to read *The Elves and the Shoemaker*?'

Chloe laughed. 'Only four.'

'You're obviously a soft touch—I bow out at twice.' He grinned at her and she smiled back.

She had a lovely smile, he thought contemplatively, perfect white teeth and a soft, sensual curve to her lips.

Chloe noticed the way his gaze rested on her lips for a second too long. The dark gaze was so intent that she felt herself tingle with awareness. Then their eyes met and she felt a delicious, shivery sensuality jolt through her body from nowhere. She couldn't have been any more surprised by the feeling than if she had reached out and touched an electric current.

As he switched off Beth's bedside lamp she turned away from him and went out into the hallway. That feeling just now was all in her imagination, she told herself crossly. Steven never looked at her with anything but the most cursory of attention. In fact, although he was always polite and respectful, she got the distinct impression that he saw her more as a piece of the office furniture than a woman.

He followed her out onto the landing. 'While we're up here I'll show you your room,' he said cordially as he led the way further down the landing and opened another door.

Chloe glanced around, noting the restful lilac colour on the walls and the white bed linen on the enormous double bed. 'Gina sometimes uses it if she has to stay over when I'm away on business. There's an *en suite* bathroom through there.' He nodded to a door at the far side of the built-in wardrobes. 'Just make yourself at home. Go and have a shower if you want…that's what I'm going to do now.'

'OK…thanks.' She smiled at him and then felt that awkward sensation of awareness again. What the hell was the matter with her? she wondered. Maybe it was just the unusual situation. She was used to standing across a desk from him, discussing work. Finding herself in a whole different environment was bound to make her a bit edgy, a bit shy of him. Possibly that was what had been wrong with her back in Beth's room as well, she realised suddenly.

'I won't be long.' As Steven headed into his bedroom Chloe made her way downstairs. There was no point having a shower now, she thought, because she had nothing to change into.

She made a pot of tea and quickly made some sandwiches with some ham she had found in the fridge earlier. Then as she waited for the tea to brew she flicked through the CDs sitting beside the small music centre. Steven had similar taste in music to her, she noticed, and on impulse she put one in the CD player and pressed 'play'.

Upstairs in his room, Steven heard the distant sound of the haunting romantic ballad and he frowned. The song that was playing had been his wife's favourite. He remembered when they had first been married how he'd used to tease her about the fact that she played it over and over again…

He saw her green eyes laughing at him.

He took off the jacket of his suit and then his tie, trying to ignore the prickling sensation that was running down his spine. Chloe was nothing like his late wife. He was just tired and Stephanie was close to his mind because of the anniversary…that was all it was.

Chloe flicked the 'repeat' button so that the song would play over again. She hadn't heard the tune in ages and it was one of her favourites. She stared out at the snow falling past the kitchen window, so white against the blackness of the sky.

She wondered where Nile was. He could at least have got in contact to explain about the money, to apologise. Surely he owed her that much?

The music snapped off behind her and she whirled around. Steven was next to the music centre.

'Sorry, Steven…was that disturbing Beth?'

'No, Beth could sleep through an earthquake.' He hesitated for a second before adding, 'I've just got a bit of a headache.'

'Probably all that paperwork today.' Chloe went across to pour the tea.

'I think I'll have something a bit stronger than tea,' Steven said, opening one of the cupboards. 'I've got a bottle of whisky in here…somewhere.'

Chloe was about to tell him that if he had a headache whisky was not the best thing to drink, then thought better of the comment. Steven didn't need her counsel.

She noticed that he had changed into jeans and a blue shirt and his hair was still damp from the shower. Chloe had never seen him dressed in such casual attire before; it suited him—made him look more boyishly attractive.

'Care to join me?' Steven asked, looking up from his perusal of the drinks cupboard.

She shook her head. 'I'll stick to the tea,' she said with a smile. 'I'm not a whisky drinker.'

'In fact, no bad habits at all?'

'I wouldn't go that far.' She wondered if there had been a dry edge to that question. Did Steven Cavendish think she was boring? The idea needled her. 'In fact, I've got more than my fair share of faults.'

His eyebrows rose. 'Name one, then?' he asked with a grin.

'I could name loads,' she retorted swiftly, 'but, as you're my boss, I don't think that would be a very good idea.'

His dark eyes glimmered with amusement. 'You're on your best behaviour around me…is that it?'

'Of course.'

He smiled and turned back to his contemplation of the cupboard. 'How about a glass of red wine, then?' He held up a bottle and looked around at her. 'Come on, help me out—am I sailing anywhere near a weakness here?'

She laughed at the absurdity of the question and then

found herself acceding. 'A glass of red wine would be nice.'

'Great; I hate to drink alone.' Steven transferred the drinks and his sandwiches onto a tray. 'Let's go and sit in the other room and relax for a moment.'

The lounge was in darkness. Chloe turned on one of the side lamps as Steven put the tray down and went over to stoke up the fire.

She sat in one of the comfortable royal-blue chairs and watched as he encouraged the dying embers in the grate then threw on a few logs. As the blaze sprang to life the flames hissed and spat greedily in the silence of the room.

'There's nothing like a real fire,' she murmured.

'There's something romantic about it, isn't there?' he agreed. 'During the day we have to keep the fireguard on because of Beth, but in the evening, when she's in bed, it's nice to sit and gaze into the flames.'

By 'we' she presumed he was referring to Helen.

He sat on the floor and opened the bottle of red wine before leaving it to warm by the flames for a moment. 'If this snow keeps up I doubt I'll be able to go to Manchester tomorrow.'

'I thought you said a little bit of snow wouldn't affect the company jet?' she reminded him light-heartedly.

He glanced up at her and grinned. 'I was wrong, wasn't I?'

'Gosh, Mr Cavendish is admitting to being wrong!' She turned laughing eyes towards the patio windows. 'Are there pigs flying around out there in that snow?'

'Less of the sarcasm, Ms Brown,' he reprimanded with a glint of humour in his eyes. 'May I remind you that according to that little speech you made in the kitchen you are supposed to be on your best behaviour around me?'

'Sorry…don't know what came over me.' With a smile

she settled herself even more comfortably in her chair. 'Must be approaching the witching hour or something.'

Steven smiled back and leaned against a chair as he poured the wine. 'Tell you what, I'm glad it is approaching the witching hour; I've seen enough of that office over these last few weeks to last me a lifetime.'

'It has been very tense in there,' Chloe agreed. She took off her glasses and put them down next to her on the coffee table.

'So let's drink to Friday, then,' Steven suggested lightly as he passed her wine across to her. 'And my wonderful PA, of course, without whom my office would disintegrate into chaos.' He raised his own glass in salute.

Smiling, she took a sip of the wine; it was warm and mellow against her throat.

For a while they sat in companionable silence. The room was in semi-darkness, and she glanced around, admiring the elegance of the decor.

All the rooms were very big in this house, possibly because it had been built in a bygone era, where style and space had been more important than practical considerations such as how much the land cost. She admired the beautifully framed watercolours on the plain cream walls, the Louis XV fireplace and the ornate marble surround, the huge mirror stretching up to the ornate coving around the high ceilings.

'You have a beautiful home,' she remarked absently.

He smiled. 'You sound as if you've never been here before.'

'Well, they have always been flying visits, haven't they? Usually when we are both so stretched with work that we've had to use every available minute to catch up with things by working from your office here.'

'Yes, I suppose you are right.' He glanced over at her

thoughtfully. 'I rely on you quite heavily sometimes, don't I?'

She shrugged. 'No more than any other boss relies on his PA.'

Steven decided that wasn't quite true. Thinking that Chloe was leaving today had made him review exactly what he had with her.

He watched the way the firelight played over her face. Her skin had a smooth, creamy quality. She looked very young, and as her eyes lifted to look over at him there was a vulnerable air about her that intrigued him. And what about her engagement ring?

'I hope I haven't disrupted your weekend too much,' he said casually. 'What were your original plans for tonight?'

'They were nothing special. I'm glad I was able to step into the breach. Did you find that list for the accounts department, by the way?'

He noted how she swiftly changed the personal question back to business. Now he came to think about it, Chloe did that a lot.

She was a wonderful PA, probably the best he had ever employed. He knew he could trust her implicitly, yet she kept herself to herself more than any other woman he had ever met.

If someone had asked him two years ago, when he'd been having problems with a personal assistant who'd had a crush on him and blushed every time he spoke to her, what his ideal PA would be he would have said someone like Chloe, someone who got on with the job and didn't have any personal interest in him. Yet perversely, now that he had exactly the right person in the job, he found himself wanting her to talk to him a bit more about something other than work. She had this kind of closed-off look about her, a 'do not touch' attitude.

'Yes, I found the list, thank you.' He took a sip of his

wine before saying slowly, 'But let's not talk about work tonight. I've had enough of that all week.'

'As work is our common denominator, there might be a few long silences if we do that.' She tried to laugh off the request, because in truth it made her feel nervously self-conscious.

Steven noted the sudden colour in her cheeks and knew he had ruffled her a little with the remark. He had no intention of overstepping the boundaries of their working relationship…for one thing, he didn't believe in mixing business with pleasure. Yet his curiosity was aroused sufficiently to want to push those boundaries aside for just a while, just to quell the sudden need to know what exactly lay behind Chloe's businesslike façade.

'Maybe we have a few other things in common that we have yet to discover,' he said lightly.

'Like a love of old houses and fine wine?' She kept her voice equally light.

'There you are, we've found two things we have in common already.'

She smiled at the teasing note in his voice. 'It does seem a bit strange for us to be relaxing like this,' she said honestly. 'I keep expecting a telephone to ring, or someone from one of the other departments to come barging in to ask for something.'

'We never get a minute's peace, do we?' Steven agreed. 'Naïvely I thought when I floated the company on the stock exchange four years ago that I'd be able to take more of a back seat. But I think I'm putting more hours in now as managing director than I ever did as the sole owner.'

'Perhaps that's the heavy price of success.' She smiled.

'Perhaps.' He took a sip of his drink.

She wondered what he was thinking about as she watched the flickering firelight playing over his features. Maybe he was remembering the heady thrill of that business deal. For a man who wasn't a chef, Steven Cavendish was a remarkably successful restaurateur.

From humble beginnings with one restaurant he had developed a style and a flair for the imaginative, setting in place the correct chef, the right location and something more…a flair for elegant dining that had struck a chord with Londoners, so that within a year the first Cavendish restaurant had been an overwhelming success and more had followed.

'I suppose I shouldn't complain. After Stephanie died I was glad to be working so many hours; it helped take my mind off things. In fact, there were points when I felt better in the office than I did at home. I had the peace of mind of knowing my mother was here with Beth…and at least at the office I could pretend everything was normal.'

'It must have been a dreadful time,' Chloe said sympathetically.

'The worst ever.'

There was silence for a moment. Steven stared into the fire reflectively. 'One of the reasons we bought this house was that we thought it was a fine family home. It has five bedrooms and we planned to fill them. Stephanie was from a big family and so am I. We both liked that and wanted the same…'

'I'm so sorry, Steven.'

The gentle sympathy of her voice jerked him from his contemplation of the past. He shrugged. 'Life goes on, Chloe. I've learnt to deal with it.'

Despite the calm tone, she knew that he had found his wife's death very difficult to come to terms with. Chloe had joined the company almost twelve months after the tragedy and she was used to a rather stern and very intense boss who could be more than a little aloof on occasion, but other members of staff had told her that before his wife had died he had been a different man, that her death had made him withdraw into himself.

Sitting here next to the fire with him, she realised that she was seeing more of that real Steven Cavendish than she had in two whole years in the office. Underneath that enigmatic cloak that he wore so well, he was a nice guy. A nice guy who just happened to be very handsome as well…she thought as she studied his rather aristocratic profile, the chiselled features, square jaw-line and the sensual curve of his lips.

He glanced over and caught her staring at him. 'What are you thinking about?' he asked lazily.

'Just…just how awful it must have been to lose someone you loved so much.'

'Yes, it was.' As he looked over at her Steven was thinking how right Chloe was—it was kind of strange to sit here talking to her like this. But the funny thing was, she was so easy to talk to. He hadn't meant to open up to her like that; in fact, he couldn't remember the last time he had talked to someone about Stephanie. He leaned over and topped up her wine glass. 'Anyway, let's not get maudlin,' he said. 'It's Friday night, reason to be celebrating.'

Realising that he might not want to talk about his wife any further, Chloe took the hint and changed the subject. 'And if this weather keeps up you might not have to go to Manchester tomorrow.' She raised her glass.

'Even if the weather improves I might find it difficult to go anyway…because by the looks of things Gina won't be back tomorrow.'

'Well, if by some miracle the weather does improve I'll stay on tomorrow and look after Beth,' Chloe offered.

'Thanks, Chloe.'

'That's OK. Beth and I get on very well together,' she said lightly. 'It would be no hardship.'

Steven smiled at her. 'Well, that's very nice of you, but

what about Nile—won't he mind?' The quietly asked question made her nerves jump. 'Where's he tonight, anyway?'

'I don't know.' She smiled a trifle over-brightly. 'Probably out drinking with his mates…' She was aware of his dark gaze moving towards her hands, to the finger that had worn Nile's ring. 'We called our engagement off almost four weeks ago,' she admitted huskily.

'Why didn't you tell me?' He frowned. 'You've never said a word about it.'

'I suppose I'm still trying to get used to the idea myself. 'And we don't really talk about our personal lives, do we?' she said. 'In fact, I had a hard time even trying to talk to you about work today.'

He grimaced. 'Sorry, Chloe; hopefully things are going to settle down soon.'

She smiled. 'We've been saying that for ages. Actually, I don't mind how busy it is—at least the days go quickly.'

'So your break-up with Nile was very sudden, was it?' He went back to the subject, his voice gently probing. 'You two have been together for a long time.'

'Yes; I met him just before I came to work for you, two years ago. But we were probably just not meant for each other. These things happen.' With massive determination she tried hard to sound as if she was very together about the whole thing, and she tilted her face up and smiled.

Steven wasn't fooled by the brave front for a minute. He noted the pallor of her skin and the bright glitter of her blue eyes. 'Just as well to find you're not suited now instead of after you married.'

'Yes…that's what I keep telling myself. But we were living together for over a year…and I did think…well, obviously I thought he was the guy for me. We'd even booked the registry office…'

'So…if it's not too personal a question…what happened? Was it another woman?'

She noted with grim amusement that his first surmise was that Nile had dumped her. 'Well, not exactly, although it turns out that there is another woman in the background now...' Maybe that other woman had been there all along and he had just picked that argument with her as an excuse to leave...and take their money, she thought grimly.

'Well, he's an idiot to give you up,' Steven said briskly. 'A complete idiot.'

The compliment took Chloe aback. She wished now that she hadn't taken off her glasses so that she could read the darkly impassive features more clearly. 'Thank you.' She looked away from him, feeling suddenly embarrassed. She couldn't really believe that she was talking like this to him; it felt really weird.

'You'll meet someone else, fall in love and thank your lucky stars that you didn't marry him.'

Her lips twisted drily. 'I didn't realise you were such a romantic.'

'Neither did I.' He smiled. 'But it sounded good, didn't it?'

Chloe thought about that for a moment and then shook her head. 'I don't know about that...'

'Why not?'

She shrugged. 'Well, this business of the earth moving and lightning zinging through you when you kiss someone—it's all just a big distraction, isn't it?'

'Distraction from what?'

'The reality of whether you really are suited to spend the rest of your life with someone.'

'You're a bit young to be so cynical.'

'I don't think it's cynical; I think it's sensible.' Chloe stared at the fire as she thought about Nile and their relationship. She had thought she had it all worked out with Nile Flynn...thought they were on exactly the same wavelength. Then came the argument four weeks ago, and she had discovered not only were they not on the same wavelength but they were tuned into entirely different frequencies.

He had accused her of being too interested in her work! It had been a ridiculous thing to say—she'd always been into her career. And, although she hadn't said it to him, she recalled all too well that he hadn't complained when he had needed her support for the long period during his own business difficulties. She had been the main breadwinner for well over a year. The strange thing was that now he was getting back on his feet financially again he seemed to hold that against her.

She would never understand men, she thought angrily. She hadn't minded helping him, had been there for him both emotionally and financially. It hadn't mattered to her who earned the most money. She had just thought that they were working in unison with the goal of their new house now well in sight.

And she had loved him; OK, there had been no wild sparks between them, there never had been. It had been more a quiet, steady kind of feeling. But Chloe had liked it like that, had liked the fact that they both had their feet on the ground; she had thought Nile felt exactly the same. He'd certainly led her to think he felt the same.

The angry rhetoric of four weeks ago had come as a total shock. It had started innocently enough because she'd been late home from work. He'd said she didn't have enough time for him. That she had all her priorities all wrong; she put her work ahead of him. She had made one little remark about the fact that she needed her job and had to treat it seriously and he had flown into a complete rage. He had made some very disdainful and derogatory remarks about her work and it was then that she had realised suddenly that he deeply resented the fact that she had been the one to keep things together financially when work hadn't been going well for him.

When she had suggested quietly that they sit down and discuss things he had arrogantly dismissed the idea and stormed out of the apartment.

It had been such a ridiculous argument that she had thought he might have reflected on the conversation, come back, sat down and discussed things in a more reasonable manner. But Nile hadn't come back, or at least not while she had been there. She had returned from work the following day and all his belongings had gone, leaving no trace that he had ever shared her life.

'I thought Nile liked the fact that I had an independent streak,' she said, turning to look at Steven. 'But it turned out that he didn't like that at all.'

For a second Steven had a glimpse of such raw vulnerability in Chloe's eyes, it was the first time he had ever seen that and it startled him slightly. Chloe was always in control, and together.

She looked away from him hastily and he was left wondering if he had imagined it.

'Anyway, I reckon the bottom line is he's seeing someone else. One of my friends saw him out with her not so long ago.' She looked back sharply at Steven. 'So much for love,' she said pointedly. 'I think the next man I meet I'm going to push that particular emotion even further down on my list of requirements.'

Steven surveyed her through narrowed, thoughtful eyes. 'So what attributes would you put at the top of your list of requirements?' he asked curiously.

'Mutual respect.' She closed her eyes for a moment as she thought about the question. 'And he'd have to be someone who is kind and thoughtful.'

Watching her, Steven couldn't help wondering if passion would figure anywhere on her list. He had a feeling that under the sensible, businesslike exterior she liked to portray she would have an extremely passionate side. His eyes drifted slowly down over her clothing. For one thing, he suspected that beneath those suits there was a very delectable body hidden away.

Aware that he was watching her with close attention, Chloe felt suddenly flustered and wondered why on earth she had told him all that! 'Anyway, that's enough about me,' she said awkwardly. 'Where's Helen tonight?' she asked, swiftly moving the conversation.

'She's been working on a very big case down at the crown court all week. Verdict came in today and her client has been acquitted. So I think the whole team are out celebrating.'

'Must be a bit difficult juggling your social life sometimes,' she considered. 'What with Helen being such a high-flying barrister and you running Cavendish.'

'It takes a bit of effort to co-ordinate our schedules,' he agreed wryly.

Outside in the hallway the grandfather clock struck two, its chimes echoing through the silence of the house.

'I didn't realise it was that time,' Chloe said in surprise.

'No, neither did I.' Steven grinned. 'For two people who don't usually talk about our personal lives, we've certainly made up on some lost ground.'

'Yes.' She smiled at him.

'And it's been very enjoyable.'

As she sipped her wine she thought how Steven was right—it was pleasurable sitting here with him like this. He was a nice guy. And there was almost something romantic about the half-light of the fire, the snow falling silently and thickly outside the patio doors. Trouble was, they were the wrong two people. He should be with Helen, she should be with Nile, she reminded herself sternly.

Her eyes moved over him contemplatively. He looked

incredibly sexy in that casual attire. She wondered suddenly
what it would be like to curl her fingers through the thick
darkness of his hair and be kissed by him. She recoiled in
shock from the thought. He was her boss! The man who
barked orders and threw paperwork at her. The man who
unnerved her with that dark, steady gaze. Had she taken
leave of her senses?

He looked over and met her eyes and smiled. It was such
a warm, attractive smile that it made her feel even more
confused. Steven Cavendish was simply gorgeous, she
thought hazily. But if he knew what she had just been
thinking he'd be horrified, she told herself.

'I'd better get to bed.' Chloe finished her glass of wine.

'We haven't finished the bottle of wine,' he said. 'Stay
and have another drink.'

'I'd better not.' She stood up and Steven also got politely
to his feet.

'Well, goodnight.' She smiled at him a little self-
consciously.

'Goodnight.' His gaze seemed to move from her eyes
towards her lips as he spoke.

Chloe didn't move away; something held her rooted to
the spot.

He reached out and smoothed a stray strand of hair away
from her eyes. It was a strangely intimate gesture and the
touch of his fingers against her skin made her feel hot inside.

'You look lovely with your hair loose like that,' he murmured. 'You should wear it like that more often.'

'It…it gets in the way.' As she stared into his eyes she
felt her heart thundering against her chest.

'You are so practical about everything,' he said gently.
'The way you dress…even the way you think about relationships.' His lips slanted into a wryly teasing smile. 'I

bet you even alphabetically index your CD collection, don't you?'

'No…' She smiled. 'But it's a very good idea…' Her voice trailed off as he leaned closer and she realised suddenly that he was going to kiss her.

She could have moved away from him, but she didn't want to. Some kind of madness seemed to take hold of her and she leaned forward, meeting him halfway and then responding to the soft pressure of his mouth with a rising feeling of hunger.

Being folded into his arms was the most amazing feeling. His lips were sensually provocative as they moved over hers, gently at first and then with a fiercer heat that set her on fire. She felt his body pressed hard against hers and it sent a thrill of excitement flooding through her. Chloe wanted to be closer; she wanted him to caress her body. When she felt his hands stroking up over her back she wanted to melt into him, feel his hands against her skin.

She wound her arms up and around his neck and the kiss deepened further, Steven exploring her mouth with a sensual mastery that sent her control spinning wildly. The sudden touch of his hands against the bare skin of her waist made her realise that her blouse had been pulled from the waistband of her skirt. The sensation of his hands against her naked skin made her tingle all over, her thoughts incoherent with a desire that was totally overwhelming.

She wanted him to unbutton her blouse, wanted to feel his hands moving and caressing over her breasts, which were now tight and aching with the weight of her desire.

He kissed the side of her face and found the soft, sensitive skin at her neck in a way that sent even more darts of pleasure through her.

If he continued like this she was going to want to make love totally and completely, and this was all wrong.

The knowledge hit her like a seed of sanity in a storm of desire.

CHAPTER THREE

As SHE stepped back from him she felt dazed and disorientated. No one had ever kissed her like that before; no one had ever turned her on so easily in such a wildly exhilarating way. Her loss of control had been scary.

'I don't suppose I should have done that,' Steven murmured huskily.

'Not the most sensible of moves,' she agreed, her voice uneven with the raggedness of her breathing. 'We've got to work together...'

His eyes lingered on her mouth again and she found herself forgetting what she was saying...where she was, even.

With the utmost difficulty she forced herself to move away. 'We'll forget it and put it down to the wine...and...and...' She couldn't think straight and her heart rate was wild, drumming chaotically with a need that was so intense it was shocking.

'And a moment of madness at a late hour,' he finished for her. In contrast to her, Steven sounded very much in control.

Sharply she tried to pull herself together. 'Yes, it was definitely madness. We'll just forget it.' It was a relief to hear her voice sounding so cool. She couldn't let him know how deeply that kiss had affected her...especially as it had just been a light-hearted, meaningless gesture to him.

Chloe turned away from him and tried surreptitiously to tuck her blouse neatly back into her skirt. She cringed as she remembered how she had wound her arms around his neck, openly inviting his caresses. How could she have behaved so shamelessly, and with her boss, of all people?

She picked up her glasses from the coffee table. As she put them back on it was as if she was slipping back behind her mask. 'Would you like me to take these dishes back into the kitchen before I turn in?' She tried to pretend that her mind had now moved away from what had happened, that she was now concentrating on practicalities.

'No, I'll see to them. I'm going to stay down here a while, finish my wine.'

'OK, well, I'll say goodnight, then.' She forced herself to turn and face him. Then remembered his response when she had said goodnight last time and wished she had just left without saying anything.

She was aware that he was watching her closely but she couldn't bear to meet his eyes. What was he thinking? she wondered... Was he just amused by what had happened? Or maybe amused by the effect it seemed to have had on her—one kiss and Chloe's thrown totally out of kilter?

'Goodnight, Chloe; sleep well.'

'Yes, I'm sure I will...I'm exhausted, actually...probably fall asleep the moment my head touches the pillow.' She wasn't going to let him think she would lose any sleep over one silly kiss.

It was a blessed relief to escape to the sanctuary of her room. She sank down on the bed and sat there for a moment, trying to steady her breathing and gather her thoughts.

Why had he kissed her like that?

A moment's madness, he had said...probably all there was to it. One thing was for certain: if they were to work as easily and comfortably together as they had in the past, she was going to have to just forget it.

She got up and went into the *en suite* bathroom to strip off and stand for a long time under the refreshing force of the power shower. Then, having no nightdress to put on, she had to slip naked between the sheets of the double bed. They were cool and refreshing against her heated skin. She reached out and switched off the bedside light, then lay staring up into the darkness.

She remembered the passion of Steven's kiss. There was no doubt about it; he was a very sexy man. She couldn't remember Nile ever being able to turn her on like that, just with a kiss. What would it be like to have Steven make love to her? she wondered. The memory of his hands moving over her skin made her body burn with a desire that alarmed her.

Turning, she buried her head into the pillow and told herself to stop thinking about it. She was only just getting over Nile; her emotions were in bits, and maybe she was even imagining the wild effect Steven had on her senses. Maybe she was on the rebound from Nile?

And anyway, whatever the truth of her feelings, Steven wouldn't be interested in her, not when he had such a glamorous girlfriend as Helen. Tonight had just been a blip; he was tired, he hadn't eaten properly…maybe he had even momentarily forgotten whom he was with.

Some time in the early hours of the morning Chloe finally fell to sleep. But her dreams were a jumbled, disturbed mix of Steven and then Nile, her body tossing fretfully as the night ticked by. When she opened her eyes she couldn't remember where she was. There was a strange silence, most unnatural to her ears, as she was used to the distant hum of the London traffic outside her apartment.

Then there was the sound of footsteps running down the hallway and a little girl giggling. And her memory returned with a whoosh. She looked at her watch. It was almost nine-thirty; she had overslept.

Chloe was about to throw the duvet back and climb out of bed when the door burst open and Beth ran in.

'Hi, Chloe.' She smiled impishly and then paused just inside the doorway as if uncertain about her welcome.

'Good morning, Beth; how are you today?' Chloe struggled to sit up whilst holding the duvet protectively around her.

Beth came further into the room. Chloe noticed she was fully dressed in a pair of jeans and a thick woollen jumper, her hair neatly in a ponytail. 'It's stopped snowing outside and Daddy says I can make a snowman.'

'Wow!' Chloe smiled at her. 'It's like Christmas, isn't it?'

Delighted with the analogy, Beth nodded and then climbed up on the bed beside her. 'Will you come and help me build him?'

Before Chloe could answer Steven appeared in the doorway. He was also dressed in jeans and a jumper. 'Beth, I told you not to go in there and wake Chloe up,' he admonished sternly.

Beth frowned and her bottom lip quivered slightly.

'It's all right, Steven, I was awake anyway,' Chloe interceded quickly.

She tried not to feel embarrassed as Steven transferred his attention away from the child to her. Suddenly she was extremely conscious of her hair, tousled and wild over the pillows, and the fact that she was wearing nothing beneath the covers.

He smiled at her, and it was a smile that did very strange things to her heartbeat. 'Morning, Chloe; how did you sleep?'

'Out like a light as soon as my head touched the pillow,' she lied cheerfully.

'Good. I'm going to fix breakfast; come down and join us when you are ready.'

'Thanks. What's the latest on your trip to Manchester?'

'I've had to cancel it. There's no way the jet would be

able to leave this morning.' He stretched out a hand to Beth. 'Come on, Beth, come out and leave Chloe to get dressed in peace.'

His daughter pointedly ignored him. 'After breakfast, will you build a snowman with me?' she asked Chloe again, her big blue eyes very wide.

'Well, I haven't really got the right clothes for going out in the snow,' Chloe said gently. 'I've only got my suit that I wear in the office.'

'Beth, I'm not going to tell you again.' Steven came further into the room.

'Oh, please, Chloe,' Beth entreated, then scrambled quickly from the bed as her father advanced. He swung her up into strong arms and she giggled. 'Please, Chloe,' she said again as he swung her over his shoulder to carry her out of the room.

'Honestly, one word from me and she does as she likes,' Steven complained wryly, but there was a glint of humour in his eyes as he looked down at Chloe. 'What about it— are you going to stay and play?'

Something about the way he said those words made her heart miss a beat, especially as she noticed his eyes dipping to the bare skin of her chest where the bedclothes had slipped fractionally down.

'I don't think you'll be able to leave for a while anyway,' he continued before she had a chance to answer. 'The snow ploughs haven't been out to clear the roads yet.' He swung away from her to carry his daughter out of the room. 'If you want some warmer clothes you might like to have a rummage in the far wardrobes. My sister usually leaves a few spare clothes here and I'm sure she wouldn't mind you borrowing them. You'd be about the same size.'

The door closed firmly behind him and she could hear Beth giggling as he carried her downstairs.

Steven's sister had to be a size smaller than her, Chloe

decided a little while later as she dried herself from the shower and then opened the wardrobes. It was flattering that Steven thought she was the same size, but he was sadly mistaken. She was about to give up her search when she found a pair of stretch jeans that looked as if they might fit. Even so, she had to lie on the bed to zip them up.

They did look good on her, though, she thought as she studied her reflection in the bedroom mirror, as did the blue cashmere jumper with the scooped neckline, which seemed to cling almost lovingly to the womanly outline of her figure. But the style wasn't really her. Because she wasn't stick-thin she tended not to wear clothes that were too revealing—not that she was ashamed of the fact that she had hips and a figure…she was just more comfortable in looser clothing that covered her up. She was contemplating taking the clothes off when there was a knock on the bedroom door.

It was Steven, and he seemed to do a double take as he looked at her, his eyes skimming over her figure in an openly assessing way that brought colour to her cheeks. 'Nice outfit,' he drawled huskily.

Before she could gather her senses to any kind of cognitive response he continued briskly, 'Nile's on the phone for you.'

'Nile!' Immediately everything else was forgotten and she felt her heart stand still, felt the colour slipping from her cheeks. 'What does he want?'

'I don't know,' Steven said sardonically. 'I didn't think it was my place to ask him.'

'No…no, of course not.' She shook her head. 'Sorry, I'm just a bit surprised that he's rung…especially here.'

'Well, he used to ring you here sometimes when you were working.'

'Yes…but we haven't spoken since he left.'

'I see. You can take it in my bedroom if you want some privacy.' Steven nodded to the door across the landing.

'Yes…OK, thanks.'

She sat down on the edge of Steven's bed and took a few steadying deep breaths before lifting the phone. It was crazy to feel nervous about speaking to Nile. He had been her partner, the man who had shared her bed over the last year…the man she had thought she would spend the rest of her life with.

'Hi, honey.' Nile's voice was subdued. 'How are you?'

'How do you think I am?' she said shakily. 'A bit shocked by your sudden departure, not to mention the other little surprises that were lurking in store for me.'

'I'm sorry, Chloe.' His voice was quietly controlled. 'I went around to the apartment last night to see you, and when you didn't answer the door I let myself in and waited. I waited all night and then I started to get worried that something had happened to you.'

Chloe felt a dart of fury. 'You walked out on me nearly four weeks ago, and suddenly you're worried about where I was last night?' Her voice was cold. 'Don't insult my intelligence any further, Nile.'

'I was really worried, Chloe. I thought you might have had an accident in that snow. I rang all of your friends and it was desperation trying your boss this morning. What are you doing over there anyway? Surely you're not working all weekend, are you?'

There was an edge to his voice that Chloe didn't like. 'That's really none of your business now,' she snapped.

'Don't be angry, Chloe…I'm sorry about the way things have turned out; I really am. I know I should have sat down and talked things through with you at the time, instead of just flying off the handle and walking out.'

'Tell me, Nile, did you walk out because of our argument, or was it because of this other woman that I've heard about?' Chloe asked.

'I haven't left you for someone else,' Nile said quickly.

'Oh, come on, Nile. My friends saw you with her last week—a cute brunette of about twenty-something ring any bells?'

There was a moment's silence and then Nile sighed. 'OK, there is someone else, but it's not a serious relationship,' he admitted cautiously. 'I just feel I need what she can offer me at the moment. She's not as strong as you…she needs me. And I quite like the way that makes me feel.'

'Well, I'm pleased for you.' Chloe couldn't help the sarcastic tone in her voice. She felt hurt.

'Look, Chloe, things have changed between us. You were a real brick carrying us through those difficulties I had financially, and I'll always appreciate it. But now I'm back on my feet I realise something about our relationship that I never did before: you don't really need me.'

'And the new woman in your life does?' she asked softly.

'Sonia is totally different to you; she's the homely type.'

'I see.' Chloe didn't know what to say to that. She felt her heart drumming uncomfortably against her chest. 'You mean she sews and bakes? Well, I don't think sewing is one of my strong points,' she admitted huskily.

'You see, you can always joke your way out of everything.' His voice sounded cross.

'What else can I do? Obviously we're just the wrong people for each other after all. But if you want a more serious approach, why have you taken all the money out of our joint bank account? The money we were saving for our wedding?'

'I've just borrowed it. I'll pay it back once I'm on my feet.'

'You cancelled all the standing orders from the bank and

withdrew cash that should have been used to pay bills.'
Chloe raked her hand distractedly through the length of her
hair. 'I'm inundated with final demands for payment.'

'Look, you'll be OK, Chlo… You've got a good job and
you're a survivor; you're strong. I'll make it all straight
with you as soon as I'm on my feet again. Meanwhile we
do need to meet to sort out our other joint finances. The
deposit we paid towards our new house—'

'As the sale won't be going through now, we'll have lost
it.' She cut across him swiftly.

'That's just it… I was thinking that maybe I'd go ahead
and buy the house on my own. I was wondering if you'd
sign it over to me?'

'And that's why you were waiting for me last night, was
it? And why you are ringing me here at my boss's house—?'

'Yes, well, this is important. There's no point us both
losing that deposit.' Nile started to speak to her as if she
was a wayward child lacking in comprehension.

Chloe was going to remind him that she was the one
who had paid the deposit on the house anyway, but stopped
herself; she had never been the type to fling things like that
in his face and she wasn't going to start now. It wouldn't
serve any purpose anyway.

'I've been to the bank and they will give me the mort-
gage on my own, so it makes sense that I should buy you
out,' he continued quickly.

'And when are you thinking of doing that?'

'I told you, as soon as I can I'll repay you everything I
owe you. But we need to sort the house out now…and
pretty quickly, because if I don't pay the next instalment
I'll lose it altogether. I need you to sign some papers—'

'I'll think about it.'

'What do you mean, you'll think about it?' He sounded
angry now.

'And in the meantime I want you to give me my front-door key back,' Chloe continued calmly.

'Look, Chloe—'

Chloe put the phone down. Then sat on the bed, looking around the room. She felt kind of lost…

What was it he had said? *You're a survivor; you're strong.* It was quite ironic that he should throw that at her as an accusation, a fault. She had to be strong; she'd had to learn how to fend for herself from a young age. And she regarded it as one of her strengths, not a weakness.

Nile Flynn had quite a cheek, saying that to her and then clearing out all their money and leaving her with debts! Justifying it by saying, Hey, it's OK, you're strong, and you're a survivor. Chloe didn't know whether to laugh or cry but she had a very cold feeling in the pit of her stomach.

She'd thought Nile was different from other men; she'd thought he was reliable. That was why she had let down her defences and eventually agreed to marry him; she had honestly believed he wouldn't hurt her. And she had worked hard at the relationship.

'Big mistake,' she whispered to herself. 'Stick to your career and forget men.'

But what about children? The question crept insidiously in on her. She wanted a family so much…the need burnt inside her. She remembered mentioning that once to Nile. He had been quite shocked. Had told her there was no way they could think about a family until they were in their new house and he was more settled in his job.

And look how things had worked out…the first thing Nile had done when he was more settled in his job was dump her. All that time she had spent carrying him, trying to be cheerful and upbeat when things weren't going right for him, and he didn't think a scrap more about her…in fact, he just resented her for it.

'Everything OK?' Steven's voice coming from the doorway startled her.

'Yes, fine.' She tried to smile, but it was a weak attempt.

Steven came further into the room and sat down on the bed beside her. 'If you want to talk about it I'm a good listener.'

'There's not a lot to say except that I've got really lousy taste in men.'

Steven smiled at that.

'You think I'm joking, but I'm not. All Nile is bothered about is that he's going to lose the deposit we've paid on a house we were buying jointly. He tried to pretend that he isn't serious about this woman he's seeing, but it sounds as if he is serious about her to me... He probably wants to move her into our new house.'

'Well, you're better off without him, Chloe. You deserve far better than that.'

Chloe couldn't find her voice to speak for a moment. Then she gave a wobbly smile as she met Steven's eye. 'Yes, my knight in shining armour will be riding up to rescue me any day now.'

Suddenly they both laughed.

'Preferably he'll arrive before my sister's wedding.'

'I didn't know you had a sister.'

Chloe nodded. 'Sinead. She's twenty-two and is really my half-sister. She's getting married in May, which is why I've booked a long weekend off that month. I'm going home to Dublin for the wedding.'

'That sounds fun.'

Chloe didn't answer.

'Why don't you come downstairs and have some breakfast?' Steven said gently.

She shook her head. 'I don't think I could eat anything. I feel a bit sick.'

'No, you don't. You're made of tougher stuff than that.'

'How do you know?' She looked over at him and he
smiled.

'I've seen you in action in the office. You're a tough
cookie.'

'That's what Nile thinks as well, but...' She was about
to tell him that it wasn't true, that it was all just an act, and
then she smiled and changed her mind. Chloe Brown would
never...ever admit to that and she wouldn't let the likes of
Nile Flynn bring her down. 'Yes...maybe you're right.'
She angled her chin up slightly.

'Of course I'm right. It's weeks since Nile left and you
haven't fallen apart. You haven't even had a day off sick
from work.'

'You can tell you're my boss! The most important thing
is that I haven't had a day off!' She shook her head but
amusement danced in her eyes for a second.

Steven grinned. 'Well, at least I've brought back a bit of
your sparkly dry humour.' He touched her face gently and
looked deep into her eyes.

Suddenly she was profoundly conscious of how close he
was sitting to her on the bed...and the touch of his hands
on her skin. She looked into his eyes and felt the laughter
still inside her, felt it being replaced by a much stronger
emotion that twisted and snaked its way through her.

'Daddy?'

Beth's voice calling from downstairs broke the intimacy
between them. Steven moved away from her. 'I'll go and
see to her,' he murmured. 'Come downstairs when you are
ready, Chloe.'

Chloe didn't immediately move to follow him. What had
just happened? she wondered. One moment she had been
thinking about Nile...the next he had been very much forgotten. Why was Steven having this effect on her? That
kiss last night had changed things between them, she
thought with apprehension. But it had just been a mistake;

she needed to forget about it, she told herself crossly, just as he had probably forgotten about it.

She sat where she was on the bed for a while, and her eyes flicked around the bedroom. It was decorated in a very masculine way, no frills or flounces, just plain walls and bedding. There was a photograph on the dresser and she crossed to have a closer look.

It was of a very beautiful woman with long golden hair and sea-green eyes; she was holding a baby in her arms, smiling tenderly down at the tiny infant. Obviously it was Steven's wife with Beth, and it had probably been taken just hours after Beth was born, judging by how tiny she was. A wave of sadness washed through Chloe. How selfish she was to feel sorry for herself because of Nile…how much worse must Steven's pain be? He had lost his wife, the mother of his child.

She put the photo down and, pulling herself sharply together, went back across to her own room.

Chloe had only intended to put on some lipstick before going downstairs, but when she looked into the mirror and noted the sensually provocative way that the jumper she was wearing clung to her figure she quickly stripped it off and dug about in the wardrobe again until she found something with a higher neck.

That's better, she thought, surveying her reflection again and noting that the grey polo-neck was longer and a bit looser, much more practical for a cold snowy day. Then she reached for her hairbrush and pinned back her hair before going downstairs.

'Sit down.' Steven nodded to where a place had been laid for her at the kitchen table next to Beth. 'Would you like tea or coffee?'

'Whatever you're having.'

'I've made both.' His eyes flicked over Chloe as he put

two pots down in the centre of the table. 'Are you OK now?'

She smiled at him. 'Yes…I'm fine.'

He opened the top oven, took out a cooked breakfast and placed it in front of her. 'There you are. Eat up—it will make you feel better.'

'Do you think you are feeding the five thousand here?' Chloe looked down at the plate of food in surprise. 'I'll be the size of a house if I eat all this. I usually just have cereal.'

'So do we during the week. But it's the weekend, time to relax a bit.' He resumed his seat opposite her. 'Besides, we have to keep our strength up to build this snowman.'

He noted that she had changed out of the attractive figure-hugging sweater into something that looked as if his sister had used it to wash the car. And once again her hair was scraped firmly back from her face into a pony-tail and she had put her glasses on.

She glanced across at him, catching him watching her quizzically, and he smiled.

'Are you going to help me build my snowman?' Beth asked happily.

Chloe looked away from Steven hastily. 'Yes, Beth, I am.'

'My best friend Rachael made one at Christmas and she put her daddy's coat and hat on it.'

It was great how having a child around lifted your spirits, Chloe thought as she reached to pour herself a mug of tea and listened to Beth's inconsequential chatter. Plus it took the edge off that feeling of self-consciousness every time she looked across and met Steven's eyes.

'Does Rachael go to your school?' Chloe asked as Beth paused for breath.

'Yes, she sits beside me. She has two brothers and a

dog…and two mummies, a stepmummy as well as her real mummy.' Beth sighed. 'She's really lucky. And her mummy has a boyfriend called Pete; he's got blond hair and he makes ice cream.'

Chloe caught Steven's eye across the table. He smiled. 'If you have finished your breakfast, Beth, you can go and find your boots, ready for going outside.'

Immediately Beth scrambled down from her chair and ran out of the kitchen.

'If she had sat there any longer you'd have got the whole of Rachael's life story,' Steven said with a grin as he reached across to refill her cup.

'You mean there's more?'

'Oh, it's a whole saga. A soap opera is boring by comparison.'

Chloe laughed and straightened the cutlery on her plate.

'Before I forget, Chloe, I've rescheduled my trip to Manchester for next Friday. I might need you to come with me.'

'That's fine. I'll put it in the diary when I get into the office on Monday.'

He looked over at her plate. 'Have you finished?'

'Yet, it was a lovely breakfast, Steven, thank you. But I couldn't eat another mouthful.'

'You're not dieting, are you?' he asked suddenly, wondering if that was why she liked to hide that beautiful body away behind shapeless clothing.

She glanced over at him with a wryly lifted eyebrow. 'No. But thanks for asking.'

He grinned at her. 'Good. I hate women who pick at their food.'

A picture of Helen Smyth-Jones rose in Chloe's mind. She was so tiny she surely wouldn't let much more than a celery stick past her lips.

Steven got up and started to clear away the dishes on the table and she stood up to help him.

He wondered if she hadn't finished her breakfast because she was so upset about Nile. Despite the brave smile as she met his eyes, she looked sad…and she had looked so lost upstairs after that phone call from him. He wanted to keep reinforcing how wrong Nile would have been for her…that she'd had a lucky escape. But he forced himself not to; maybe it wasn't what she needed to hear right now.

'So, tell me more about your sister's wedding,' he asked instead.

'There's not much to tell. I think it's going to be quite a big affair and I'm chief bridesmaid.' She pulled a face. 'I'm just hoping they haven't chosen a dress for me that's completely hideous. I've got this picture in my mind of something pink and frilly that will make me look dreadful.'

'You'd look quite fetching in something pink and frilly, I'm sure.' Steven smiled.

'No, trust me, I wouldn't,' Chloe said firmly. 'But it's Sinead's big day and I've told her I'll go with whatever she wants…also I haven't been home in a long time, so I've got to go with the flow.'

'I didn't know you were originally from Ireland,' Steven said. 'But now I listen to your voice I can hear the faint accent.'

'Well, I'm not really from Ireland. When I was little we lived in London, then Mum and Dad got a divorce and Dad went to live in Ireland.' Chloe closed the dishwasher and leaned back against it to look over at him. 'Then when Mum died I went to live with my dad and his wife Margaret, who is from Dublin.'

'How did your mother die?'

'Car accident.'

'I'm sorry, Chloe; that must have been very tough for you. How old were you when that happened?'

'Let's see…I was six when Dad left, so I was eleven when I went to Ireland.'

'And do you get on with your stepmother?'

Chloe nodded. 'Yes, she's lovely. She helped me come to terms with a lot of things. '

'It sounds like you've been through some tough times?'

Chloe hesitated for a second. 'Yes, but kids bounce back.' She smiled, and didn't tell him just how tough those times had been. Especially those years after her father had left. Sometimes when she looked back she thought those were the years that had shaped her. She had watched her mother and had learnt all about pain at first hand. Nile had accused her of being too strong…in her book there was no such thing as being too strong.

She had made up her mind long ago to be as self-reliant as possible. It was her safety net and she wouldn't give that part of her character up, for Nile or anyone else.

'I suppose you are right—children are resilient. Yet I worry about Beth, about the fact that she has no mother.'

'She seems very well-adjusted.' Chloe looked over at Steven. 'Do you think she remembers her mother?'

Steven shook his head. 'No. Any memories she has are the ones I've passed down to her. Little things like how much her mum loved her.'

'That's not such a little thing.' Chloe smiled over at him.

She liked Steven more than she could say at this moment. His tenderness and his love for his daughter struck a chord with her deep inside.

'She's lucky to have such a good dad and she obviously adores you. Last night, for instance…she knew Gina was worried about her dad and it started her worrying about you.'

'Did it?'

Chloe nodded. 'Just for a little while she was distressed,

thinking it was you who had been taken to the hospital. I used to feel worried like that about my mum.'

'But you had your dad as well, even though they were divorced.'

'He was a long way away… And at the time…I didn't really know if he wanted to see me at all.'

Steven looked over at her. Although the words were firmly spoken, he sensed the unhappiness, the powerless feeling of a child unable to reach out to a parent.

He was going to deepen his questions but Beth came running back into the room, dressed in woolly scarf and wellington boots, and the moment was lost.

'I think you need a coat, Beth.' Chloe laughed. 'But you look great. Come on upstairs and I'll organise you.'

Happily the little girl tucked her hand in Chloe's. 'I've got a pink coat and a blue one. Will you put my hair up in a pony-tail like yours?'

'Yes, of course I will.' Chloe smiled. 'We won't be long, Steven,' she said over her shoulder.

'That's OK, take your time.' Steven watched as they went out of the room. Chloe was good around his daughter…she had a kind of easy, natural warmth. Obviously that was why Beth was responding so well to her.

All in all Chloe was quite a revelation, he thought in bemusement. And as for that kiss last night—that had totally blown his mind. He had only meant to brush her lips gently with his, but once he had kissed her he hadn't been able to draw back. He'd wanted to kiss her again today; it was as if some sort of spell had fallen over him. But, whatever it was, something had very definitely changed between them this weekend.

CHAPTER FOUR

THE garden was shrouded with a thick blanket of virgin snow. It lay across the bare dark branches of the trees and the plants like icing sugar and it decorated the eaves of the house with a lacy canopy against a jewel-blue sky.

Although the sun was shining, it did little to relieve the glacial current in the air. Chloe stamped her feet to try and keep them warm as she stepped back and watched Beth put the finishing touches to her snowman.

'He looks great,' Steven called from beside her, his voice warm with encouragement. 'Just tilt his hat a little, give him a more jaunty look.'

Beth pushed the black trilby sideways.

'He looks drunk now,' Chloe laughed. 'Where did that hat come from? It's not yours, is it, Steven?'

'No. I don't know whose it is. It's been hanging in the vestibule for months.' He grinned at her, and then noticed the way she was stamping her feet and rubbing her hands. 'Are you cold?'

'Only because I'm standing still. I was OK while we were working on old Mr Snowy.'

'I should have found you some gloves to wear.'

'I'm enough of a charity case as it is,' Chloe laughed. 'I've got your sister's clothes on, and Gina's wellington boots. The only thing that's mine is this black duffel coat. I must look a sight.'

For a second Steven's eyes drifted over her appearance in a swift appraisal, making her feel acutely awkward. 'You look very nice, although I think I preferred the first jumper you put on this morning.'

'Did you?' Chloe tried to sound nonchalantly indifferent to his preferences. 'It wasn't very suitable for being out in the cold.'

'Do you ever wear contact lenses?' he asked suddenly, his voice curious.

'Sometimes. But in all honesty I prefer wearing my glasses.' She kept her gaze firmly centred on Beth as she spoke.

'Just like you prefer to tie your hair back?'

'I suppose so. It's tidy and—'

'Practical,' Steven supplied with a smile.

She remembered last night and how he had told her he preferred her hair loose…how he'd kissed her. She felt her heart thump with an awareness of him that seemed to swamp her.

'Actually, you suit your glasses,' he said suddenly.

His sudden interest in her appearance perplexed her. He was probably just making polite conversation but she wished he would look away from her. As his gaze rested on her lips the memory of his kiss struck through her with a suddenness that brought an inner central heating. She rubbed her hands together with even more ferocity, trying to stamp out the thoughts.

'Have you heard anything from Gina?' She moved the conversation away from herself.

'Yes, she phoned me early this morning. Apparently her dad has been taken off the critical list at the hospital.'

'Oh, I am pleased.'

'Yes, it's good news,' Steven said. 'The only bad bit is that she gave her notice in to me. She says she wants to be able to look after him herself.'

'So is she leaving straight away?'

'No, she'll be here as usual Monday morning. Her father is going to be transferred to a nursing home for a while because he needs specialised care. She wanted to give me plenty of notice so that I could find someone else as soon as possible.'

'She's a nice girl.'

'Yes, she is, and I wish she wasn't leaving. Beth is very attached to her.'

Chloe glanced over and caught the worried look in Steven's eyes as he watched Beth playing happily around the snowman. 'You'll find someone else, Steven.'

'I know.'

'And at least your mum lives near by.'

'Yes, Mum is wonderful, but I don't want to put on her too much.' Steven raked a hand through the darkness of his hair. 'Anyway, I'll just have to get on to that agency we used last time…perhaps you'd give them a ring on Monday?'

'Of course; do you want me to do the same as last time and carry out the preliminary interviews? Whittle down the list of applicants for you?'

Steven smiled. 'Whatever would I do without you, Chloe?' The gentleness of his tone was quite unlike any way he usually spoke to her about work.

'I'm sure you'd manage perfectly.' She glanced up at him and he smiled. A smile that seemed to shut out the cold of the day and start a fire inside her.

'I'm not entirely sure about that at all, Chloe,' he said, and she wasn't sure if he was teasing her or being serious.

Beth stumbled in the snow as she stepped backwards to look at her snowman and Chloe took the opportunity to move away from Steven and help her back up on her feet.

'Are you OK, sweetheart?' she asked as she brushed the snow off the little girl's coat.

'Yes…' Beth giggled. 'I wish it would snow all the time—it's great.'

Chloe smiled, her eyes moving over the cute dimples in

Beth's cheeks as she laughed. 'You'd get fed up if it snowed all the time.'

'No, I wouldn't!' Beth shook her head. 'You could come every weekend and help me build a snowman.'

'Looks like you've got a fan,' Steven said with a grin as he walked over to join them.

'Yes…' Chloe watched as Beth ran back to her snowman. 'I'm a big fan of Beth as well.' It was strange, but there was something about Beth that just made her want to give her a big hug. Upstairs in the bedroom as she had brushed the little girl's hair she had listened to her chatter and wondered what it would be like to have a child like her. To live with a man like Steven…be part of their family. It had been a passing, fleeting daydream…incredibly unrealistic, but for a moment quite pleasurable. 'She's very sweet, Steven.'

'Adorably gorgeous,' Steven agreed wryly. 'Except when she's naughty, as Gina would probably testify.'

Chloe smiled.

The phone rang inside the house and Steven excused himself to go and answer it.

When he returned Beth and Chloe were in the middle of a snowball fight. He stood and watched for a moment, grinning at Chloe's antics as she chased Beth, who was giggling breathlessly, around and around the snowman.

Then he joined in the fun. They were all laughing so much they didn't hear a woman's voice calling Steven's name. It was only when a snowball that Chloe threw at Steven went astray, whizzing over his head and hitting Helen squarely on the chin, that they realised that she was there.

Steven glanced around, saw what had happened and laughed. His girlfriend, however, did not look one little bit amused.

'I'm really sorry, Helen,' Chloe said, horrified by the

thunderous expression on the other woman's face. 'It was an accident.'

Helen didn't reply immediately; she was too busy brushing the snow from her face and her black cashmere coat. Her dark hair swung silkily back into its long bob as she looked up again towards Chloe, dark eyes narrowing on her. But she said nothing.

Chloe found herself remembering the way she and Steven had kissed last night and guilt shot through her. It had been a moment of madness and at least they had both had the sense to realise that...and pull away from the situation. She tried to make herself feel better with the thought, but the guilt wouldn't go away.

'Can we play some more, Daddy?' Beth asked plaintively.

'Maybe later, honey,' Steven grinned. 'Now, remember your manners and say hello to Helen.'

'Hello, Helen.' Beth shuffled from foot to foot and barely glanced at Helen. Chloe noted that Helen's response was equally lukewarm. However, her welcome to Steven was anything but half-hearted—as he walked across to her she reached up and kissed him full on the lips.

Chloe averted her eyes, feeling an awkward twist of something deep inside. It was a really odd feeling, one that she had never experienced before, and she couldn't quite get a handle on it. It couldn't be embarrassment because the kiss wasn't that steamy...just tenderly possessive. Maybe what she was feeling was the sting of reality...certainly, seeing Helen with Steven like this slammed the door closed on those stupid fantasies she'd had that he was in any way interested in her...and that crazy daydream she had indulged in just for a moment of being a part of this family seemed to mock her now.

'Shall we go inside and have a drink?' Steven suggested lightly as he pulled back from Helen.

'That would be nice.' Helen smiled up at him.

'I should be going,' Chloe said as she walked with them back into the house. 'Obviously the roads are cleared now.'

'Yes, the snowploughs have been out and the roads are fine,' Helen said. 'We won't detain you if you want to get off.'

'Don't go, Chloe,' Beth piped up from beside her. 'I want you to play outside with me and Daddy again.'

'Chloe hasn't got time for that now, honey.' Steven ruffled the top of the child's hair, and then glanced over at Chloe. 'But have a coffee with us before you head back to the city,' he said. He didn't wait for her answer but disappeared into the kitchen to put the kettle on, Beth trailing in his wake.

Chloe kicked off her wellington boots, hung her coat up and followed Helen into the lounge. The other woman was flicking through a magazine that had been lying on the coffee table; she barely glanced up as Chloe sat down in the chair next to the fire.

'The weather has been awful, hasn't it?' Chloe said politely as Helen flicked over a few more of the glossy pages. 'You'd never think it was April.'

'No, you wouldn't.' She didn't glance up immediately, and when she did her gaze flicked derisively over Chloe's attire.

It was no wonder she was looking at her with such disdain, Chloe thought. Next to Helen's well-groomed, chic appearance, she probably looked a sight.

Everything about Helen was perfect, Chloe thought. Her figure was probably a size eight and her clothes were obviously designer; the smart skirt hugged her slender hips and her flat stomach and stopped just at the knee, revealing beautiful, long, shapely legs, well-shod in soft kid-leather boots.

The silence between them seemed to stretch and Chloe

searched for something else to fill it. 'I was minding Beth for Steven last night and I got stranded here because of the snow.'

'Yes, Steven told me.' Helen put the magazine down, glanced at her watch and stifled a yawn.

Chloe decided to give up. Helen never spoke very much to her when she popped into the office or, for that matter, when she phoned to speak to Steven. She was always cool and reserved.

Steven came back in with the tray of coffee and suddenly Helen seemed to come to animated life again. 'Darling, we had a wonderful time last night. It's a pity you couldn't have stayed in town; we went clubbing to La Ruba.'

'Well, like I said to you on the phone, I had a meeting and then Gina had to dash off. It was a bit chaotic. In fact, it would have been a disaster if Chloe hadn't waded in to the rescue.' He smiled across at Chloe as he handed her the mug of coffee and then sat down beside Helen on the settee.

'I didn't mind at all,' Chloe said easily. Beth came into the room and went over to sit on the arm of Chloe's chair. 'We had good fun last night, didn't we, Beth?' Chloe said.

Beth nodded and slipped further down so that she was sitting on Chloe's knee. 'We played tiddly-winks and Chloe read me a story.'

'Lovely.' Helen's smile didn't quiet reach her eyes as she watched Beth cuddling in beside Chloe on the chair. 'Watch you don't knock Chloe's coffee, darling,' she said. 'We don't want coffee all over the chair, do we? Why don't you come and sit next to me?' She patted the space on the settee on the other side of her.

Beth shook her head. 'I won't knock Chloe's coffee.'

'So where else did you get to last night?' Steven asked Helen.

'We had a meal and a few drinks before the club…Henry and Jason were there. They said to tell you hi.'

Chloe was distracted from the conversation as Beth leaned her head against her arm. She glanced down at the child. Her cheeks were very flushed and her eyes looked a bit heavy. 'Are you tired, Beth?' Chloe asked quietly. Beth nodded.

'Henry was such a hoot. He got us into the VIP lounge at La Ruba and we drank champagne all night…'

'Sounds fun.' Steven's eyes flicked over towards Beth. He watched as Chloe pressed her palm against the child's forehead, then put her arm around her and whispered something against her ear, something that made Beth smile.

'…Henry has invited us to his lodge in Hampshire for a weekend party next Friday…there's a clay-pigeon shoot and we can go riding…what do you think?'

'I'm sorry, Helen, but I've got to go to Manchester on business on Friday.'

Helen frowned. 'We can go Saturday morning, I suppose…'

'Well, we'll see. I've got a few complications with Gina's dad being ill.'

Watching Helen's face from across the room, Chloe could see that the answer did not please her.

'Well, can't you find someone else?' she asked. 'How hard can it be to find someone to look after a six-year-old for the weekend?'

Hurriedly Chloe finished her coffee, deciding it was time to go.

'I'll just get my belongings from upstairs, Steven,' she said, disentangling herself carefully from Beth.

Beth followed her as she stood up. 'I'm not six until next week,' she told Chloe as they went out of the door.

'I know, darling. What do you think you'll get for your birthday?'

'I asked Dad to buy me a magic set.'

As Chloe closed the door on the lounge she clearly heard Helen saying, 'Chloe is such a plain girl, isn't she? Such a shame for her.'

Steven's reply was lost behind the closed door.

Chloe frowned to herself as she went upstairs. Who the hell did Helen Smyth-Jones think she was anyway? she thought angrily.

'And Aunty Maddi is going to get me a water gun.'

'Gosh, you'll have fun with that,' Chloe said. With a bit of luck you might fire it at Aunty Helen, she thought as they went upstairs together.

She folded her business suit. There was no point changing back into it, as she would have to wash these jeans before returning them to Steven. She lifted her handbag and then glanced at herself in the mirror.

Such a shame for her... Helen's derisive and cutting words played over in her mind. She wondered what Steven's reply had been.

Not that she gave a damn, Chloe thought furiously.

She looked over at Beth, who was watching her from the open doorway.

'I wish you didn't have to go,' Beth said despondently.

There was something about the way the little girl looked at her with those big blue eyes that made Chloe's heart go out to her.

She went across to give her a hug. 'I'm afraid I have to go, honey, but I'll see you soon, I'm sure,' she whispered.

There were more important things in life than looks anyway, Chloe thought as she pulled away from the warmth of Beth's body. If Helen Smyth-Jones was really serious about Steven she could do with transferring some attention away from her own appearance to concentrate instead on building a relationship with his daughter.

For a moment she found herself thinking about her stepfather. She hadn't mentioned Michael when she had been telling Steven about her parents' break-up.

Michael Blake was someone she preferred to forget. He'd been very good-looking, suave and sophisticated. And her mother had adored him, would have done anything for him. Chloe had watched helplessly from the sidelines as he had destroyed her. Insidiously menacing, he had almost seemed to enjoy the reign of fear he had waged over them.

He had hated Chloe. As a six-year-old, she hadn't been able to understand why...even now she didn't understand what made the likes of Michael Blake tick. All she knew was that it had taken a long time for the nightmares to go away, and sometimes even now when she closed her eyes she could still see him.

CHAPTER FIVE

CHLOE went into the office earlier than usual on Monday morning to make sure everything was in place for the board meeting at nine. She was in the boardroom, placing an agenda at each place setting, when Steven arrived.

'Crikey, did you sleep here last night or something?' he said, glancing at his watch.

She smiled. 'I'm only here ten minutes before you. Just thought I'd get ahead with things before everyone arrives for the meeting.'

Steven looked at her closely. As usual she was perfectly groomed; she was wearing a vanilla suit and a round-neck silk top in a matching colour, and her hair was drawn back from her face, but not as tightly as usual, and a few tendrils had escaped to curl provocatively around her face. Her make-up was perfect. But behind the confident façade he could see she looked drawn and tired. 'Couldn't you sleep last night?'

She contemplated lying and then gave up the idea as she met the darkness of his eyes. 'No...not really.'

As she finished distributing the papers down the long polished table he noticed that she was wearing higher heels than normal; they were very trendy shoes, smart, but somehow there was something provocative about them. Maybe it was the fact that they seemed to emphasise her small, shapely ankles.

'What about you—how did the rest of your weekend go?'

Steven tore his eyes away from her feet. 'I've had better days,' he said, opening his briefcase to put some of his own notes down at the top of the table. 'I tried to break it gently to Beth that Gina will be leaving soon.'

'She didn't take it well?'

Steven looked grim for a second. 'She cried so hard she almost made herself sick.'

Chloe cringed. 'It must have been awful.'

'Yes, it was. And it wasn't helped by Helen suggesting I send her away to boarding-school.' He noted the shocked expression on Chloe's face.

'She didn't suggest that in front of Beth, did she?' Chloe was aghast.

'No…she's not that insensitive.' Steven grinned wryly. 'She suggested it quietly to me a bit later on Sunday afternoon.'

One of the receptionists knocked on the door and put her head around. 'Two of the managers have arrived for the meeting, Mr Cavendish,' she said briskly. 'They're in Reception.'

'Right.' Steven nodded at the woman. 'I'll be out in a minute.'

'You're not seriously considering sending Beth to boarding-school, are you?' Chloe asked immediately as the door closed again. 'She's so young!'

'Yes, she is,' Steven agreed, and then shook his head. 'I told Helen that there's no way I'd ever consider it,' he said forcefully. 'But she thinks I'm out of line. Apparently, both she and her brother went to boarding-school from a very young age. She thinks it's a great idea.'

'Well, maybe that was all right for Helen, but it wouldn't be for Beth, not when she's lost her mother. She relies on you to make her feel secure and wanted, Steven. That's very important in her circumstances.'

Steven met her eyes and noted the earnest expression in them. He wondered if she was drawing on her own experiences as a child; there was such a lot of passion in that plea, totally unlike Chloe's usual composed demeanour. 'I'm in complete agreement,' he said. 'Helen and I did not part on good terms yesterday.'

'Because you didn't agree with her about a boarding-school?'

'That and the fact that I can't go away with her next weekend.' Steven closed his briefcase with a sharp, decisive click. 'But the timing is off. I can't go away for a weekend enjoying myself when I've got a little girl feeling sad at home. I have to put Beth's happiness and welfare first…over my own happiness…but Helen just can't understand that. I think it spells the end of the road for our relationship.'

'I'm sorry, Steven; that must be really hard,' Chloe said quietly.

There was another knock on the door and the receptionist put her head around again. 'Ms Smyth-Jones is on the phone for you, Mr Cavendish,' she announced cheerfully.

'OK, I'll take it in my office.' Steven looked back at Chloe. 'I'd better speak to her. Will you deal with whoever is in Reception? I won't be long.'

'Sure.' Chloe watched him go and wondered what Helen was ringing to say…maybe she would apologise. If she had any sense she would. Steven was an honourable man, trying to do the best for his daughter. It was one of the things she loved about him…or, rather, liked about him, she corrected herself with a frown.

It was about fifteen minutes before Steven came back, and by that time most of the other directors had arrived and Chloe had shown them into the boardroom. They were chatting amiably with her, drinking coffee around the table.

'Sorry to keep you waiting, gentlemen,' Steven said as he shook hands all around. He was urbane and businesslike as he took his seat at the top of the table. Chloe wondered what had transpired between him and Helen. She hoped fervently that he had not backed down.

But there wasn't time to think about it as the last of the directors arrived and the business of the day began.

It was late in the afternoon before the meeting ended and Chloe's wrist ached from the writing of the minutes she had taken. As she tidied her notes and got up to collect the folders from the table one of the directors from the Scottish head office came over to speak to her.

'Just wanted to say how impressed I was with the way everything ran so smoothly today, Chloe.' He smiled warmly at her. 'If you ever get fed up working in England, there would be a place for you in my office north of the border any day. I really could do with a treasure like you organising everything.'

Before Chloe could answer Steven broke from his conversation with someone else and glanced over with a frown. 'Excuse me, Cliff, but poaching staff is not permitted here,' he said, his tone light-hearted. 'You'll have to find your own treasure.'

Cliff laughed. 'Sorry, Steven…that was a bit out of order, wasn't it? Just couldn't help myself.' He placed a business card down on top of Chloe's notes. 'I'm going to be in London for a few more days,' he said to Chloe with a twinkle in his eye.

She smiled at him. Cliff Roberts was a nice guy, about ten years older than Steven, with greying hair and a distinguished air. 'Thanks,' she said blithely. 'I'll put the card in my filing system.'

As the last of the directors left the building Steven walked with them out to the front reception area. Chloe was tidying away the last of the crockery from lunch when he returned to the boardroom.

'Well, I'm glad that's over,' he said as he closed the door. She looked around with a smile. 'I thought it went well.'

'Yes, it did…but I didn't think it would go on this long. You must be exhausted taking all those notes, Chloe.'

'No, I'm fine,' she lied cheerfully.

'The refreshments you ordered were a stroke of genius.' He walked across and picked up the card that Cliff had placed on the table for her. 'Cliff was right about the way you handled everything; the presentation was faultless,' he remarked. 'But he had a damn nerve trying to poach you away right under my nose.'

'You make me sound like a fish being reeled in.' Chloe grinned. She finished stacking the folders and glanced across at him. 'He seems quite a nice guy, though. I was rather flattered.'

Steven didn't look amused. 'Well, don't be. Cliff Roberts has something of a reputation with women. He got divorced last year and according to the grapevine he's had more affairs in that time than hot dinners.'

'Really?' Chloe shook her head. 'I didn't know. But that wasn't why he was giving me his card. I think it was just a bit of fun and he's probably genuinely looking for a PA.'

'You must be joking,' Steven muttered. 'He couldn't take his eyes off you all the way through the meeting.'

'Couldn't he?' Chloe was astounded by the remark. 'I think you are imagining things, Steven.'

'And I think you can be a bit naïve, Chloe,' Steven muttered with a shake of his head.

The remark irritated Chloe.

'I'll destroy this card, shall I?' he continued nonchalantly.

'No, thank you!' Chloe whipped it from his hand as she walked past. 'I'll do it.'

Steven watched as she put it in the pocket of her suit. She smiled at him. 'You never know…maybe he'd like to go to a wedding in Ireland,' she added mischievously.

She was only joking, but Steven looked less than amused.

What had happened to his sense of humour? Chloe wondered as she left the room.

The working day was drawing to a close. Steven drummed his fingers on his desk and tried to concentrate on the report in front of him, but his mind kept wandering and so did his eyes. His office door was open slightly and through the opening he could see Chloe sitting at her desk.

She was doing some audio typing and was concentrating very hard on the task. He noticed how straight she sat in her chair. A shaft of spring sunshine came in through the window behind her, highlighting the blonde lights in her hair, giving it a kind of a halo effect—or maybe it was just the way the headphones she was wearing disturbed her hair… Whatever it was, she looked like an angel in the late-afternoon glow.

He smiled at the fanciful thought and tried to return his attention to his work. But he couldn't concentrate. Something wouldn't let him. He thought about the board meeting earlier, remembered the way Cliff Roberts had kept looking at Chloe. Then he remembered Chloe's wisecrack about asking him to her sister's wedding. She had to be kidding…didn't she? Chloe was too vulnerable at the moment to be able to deal with the likes of Roberts.

He stood up and walked through to her office, although he had no idea why on earth he was going in there. It was as if he was being magnetically drawn.

Chloe looked up from her typing and was surprised to see Steven standing in the doorway, watching her. She whipped off the headphones. 'Sorry? Did you want something? I couldn't hear with this tape.'

'No, I didn't want anything, I just…' He trailed off before saying firmly, 'I just wondered if you would have a drink with me after work.'

He watched her eyes widen in surprise. It was no wonder she was looking astounded; he was feeling a bit shell-shocked himself. He hadn't walked out here with the intention of asking her that, yet he had just opened his mouth and the words had come…almost of their own volition.

'I just thought, as you are interviewing childminders for me tomorrow…we could discuss the kind of hours I'll need and the qualities I'm going to be looking for…' He tacked the excuse on as a hurried afterthought. 'And I thought we may as well talk about it over a relaxing drink.'

'Oh…right.' She glanced at her watch. 'I'm supposed to be going out tonight…'

'Well, if you are busy…' He frowned and wondered where she was going. Surely she hadn't phoned Cliff Roberts that fast? Then again, Cliff was only going to be in London for the next couple of days. So maybe she hadn't seen the point of hanging around.

'I could probably spare you an hour, if that's OK?' she said casually now.

'An hour…' Steven nodded. 'That's fine.'

Chloe watched as he disappeared back into his office, closing the door behind him. Now, what was that all about? she wondered. Never in the two years she had worked here had Steven asked her out for a drink after work. Even when she'd been interviewing nannies for him last time. As she recalled, he had just handed her a list of the hours he wanted and the type of person he was looking for and that had been that until he had personally interviewed the people she had placed on her short list.

She frowned and wondered if she had done the right thing telling him she was going out tonight; she wasn't really—it had just been the first thing that had come into her mind, a kind of defensive impulse.

She put her headphones back on and tried to concentrate once more on her work.

Chloe was used to being one of the last people to leave the Cavendish premises at the end of the day. There was nothing very different about walking through the deserted offices with Steven, watching as he flicked out the lights and locked up. And yet there was something different…something in the air…a feeling, a tension, which she couldn't quite understand. Maybe it was all in her mind because he had casually asked her to join him for a drink?

They stepped into the lift and Steven pressed the button for the car park in the basement. There was silence between them as it plummeted. Chloe glanced at her boss's reflection in the mirrored walls. He was wearing a dark overcoat thrown over the top of his dark business suit. The pristine whiteness of his shirt and the vivid blue of his tie contrasted dramatically with his dark hair and dark eyes. She wondered idly if he had any Italian blood in him. He looked Latin sometimes. Steven glanced up and caught her watching him in the mirror and smiled. She smiled back politely and hastily averted her gaze.

Steven was used to women gazing at him in admiration; she had seen the effect he had on the other women in the office, who practically swooned as he walked by. But she didn't want to be one of the fawning throng. She had to keep her feet firmly on the ground around him, otherwise her work would be compromised.

Up until last weekend that hadn't been a problem. Steven was always so businesslike that she had never really looked at him in any light other than 'the boss'.

But now the sands of that formal relationship seemed to have shifted slightly. Whether it was because she had spent some time with him at the weekend and found him to be a warm and fun person…or whether it was that kiss…that small indiscretion that they had brushed off as just a momentary madness... She didn't know.

Foolish mistake or not, that kiss kept popping into her mind at the most inopportune moments; like now, for instance.

She needed to get a grip, she told herself angrily. She wanted back to the uncomplicated business approach they had shared before—or did she? she suddenly asked herself. Yes, of course she did, she reinforced; she didn't want an affair with her boss, and anyhow the gorgeous Helen was in his life. All right, they had been going through a rough patch in their relationship, but it was probably merely a hiccup...for all she knew, they had made it up on the phone this morning. As for her, she wanted an uncomplicated life for herself in the future; romantic notions about her boss were not on her agenda.

The lift doors swished open and she took a deep breath of air, glad to be out of the confined space with him.

Like the office block above, the car park was completely empty. Steven pressed a button and his black BMW automatically unlocked. Their footsteps echoed in the vaulted silence as they walked across towards it.

He tossed his briefcase onto the back seat as she walked around to the passenger side.

'Are you hungry, Chloe? We could get something to eat together.'

'Sorry?' She glanced blankly at him and their eyes met over the roof of the car.

'I said, are you hungry?' he replied patiently.

She'd heard him perfectly well the first time; she just couldn't work out what was going on here. This was way out of their normal territory.

'As we just had a working lunch, due to that board meeting, I thought it might be pleasant to go home via the Waterside? What do you say?'

The Waterside was one of the most exclusive restaurants in the Cavendish chain. Although Chloe had visited it many times on her own for work purposes, she had never eaten there.

'Have you got a business appointment there or something?'

'No. This has nothing to do with work,' Steven said impassively. 'I just thought it was the one restaurant where I'd be assured to get a good table at short notice. But we can go somewhere else if you'd prefer?'

'No…' Suddenly Chloe remembered her lie…she was supposed to be going out somewhere later. 'I think we'd better stick with the pub, because I've really only got an hour.'

'Fine…whatever you want.' He smiled at her and they got into the car.

There was silence between them as he started the engine and drove out onto the busy London streets.

Chloe watched as he skilfully manoeuvred the car through the rush-hour traffic. It was a pleasant day; a watery spring sun had dispersed the snow, and the promise of better weather suddenly lurked around the corner.

'Did you sort out your differences with Helen this morning?' She tried to ask the question nonchalantly, but the truth of the matter was that curiosity was killing her.

'Not really.' Steven darted a glance at her. 'We've decided to finish things.'

'Oh! I'm sorry.' She said the words politely, yet at the same time she wondered if they were strictly true. She wasn't quite sure how she felt about that piece of information. There was a part of her that thought, Good! Helen Smyth-Jones didn't deserve Steven and Beth…how could she, when she had suggested something as awful as sending Beth away?

'Well, don't be too sorry,' Steven said drily. 'If I'm

truthful I think it's been on the cards for a while. Maybe if I had been a bachelor things would have worked out...but a widower with a small child was never really Helen's ideal partnership. We spoke very candidly on the phone this morning, and I think we both felt better for it. It was all very amicable. She even said herself that she would never have made a good stepmum, and really if I get married again that is a priority for me.'

'Yes, of course.' Chloe looked over at him, very impressed by that sentiment. There were times when she liked Steven Cavendish...so much.

'But it's good that we can remain friends because I do think highly of her,' Steven continued as he swung the car into a pub car park. 'Is here OK?' he asked.

She looked up and noticed it was the Rose and Crown, her local. Virtually around the corner from where she lived. 'Yes, fine.'

The bar was packed with people who had just finished work. The background music from the jukebox was drowned out by the hum of conversation and the occasional tone of a mobile phone ringing. They jostled their way through the crowds of people in business suits and then Steven spied a seat in the corner. 'You go and sit down and I'll bring the drinks,' he said. 'What would you like?'

'White wine, thanks.'

He nodded and disappeared towards the bar while she headed in the other direction.

She sat down and watched the buzz at the bar. It was surprising how busy it was for a Monday. Chloe rarely came in here midweek. Sometimes she had met Nile for an after-work drink here, but only on a Friday, when they had both been able to relax.

Because Steven was almost a head taller than most of the other men at the bar he seemed to get served faster. Chloe was so deeply absorbed watching some women a little further down from him, eyeing him up with interest, that she jumped when a familiar voice spoke her name.

'Hello, Chloe; fancy seeing you here on a Monday!'

Chloe turned and saw her friend Gillian sliding into the seat beside her. Gillian lived in the apartment across the hall from her. She was about the same age as Chloe, a stunningly attractive redhead with the most gorgeous figure.

'How are you?' Gillian smiled. 'You don't usually come in here midweek?'

'No, well…it was a spur-of-the-moment decision.' Chloe smiled. 'Where's Brian—is he not with you?' Brian was her equally attractive partner.

'Playing football. I'm with Samantha…you know, who works with me at the bank. She's here somewhere—don't ask me where. You're not here with Nile…are you?' Gillian was scanning the bar.

'No. There is no going back, Gill,' Chloe said firmly. 'It really is all over.'

Gillian pulled a sympathetic face. 'I still can hardly believe it.'

Chloe shrugged.

'Who are you here with, then?'

'Just my boss; he's at the bar, getting the drinks.' Chloe nodded over towards Steven.

'Which one is he?' Gillian asked, following her gaze.

'Tall guy with dark hair.'

Gillian's eyes widened. 'Not that gorgeous Adonis?'

Chloe smiled. 'Yes, he is good-looking, isn't he?' she said.

'Well, put it this way—I wouldn't kick him out of bed.' Gillian looked back at her with admiration. 'Wow!'

'It's just a business drink,' Chloe found herself saying hastily.

'Really? Well…all I can say is, grab him quick. Is he single?'

'Yes, but—'

'No buts, he's gorgeous.'

'He's my boss, Gill, and anyway he's not really my type…' She cut her words off in mid-sentence as a glass of wine was placed before her. She glanced up, directly into Steven's eyes, and felt her heart miss a beat.

'Who's not your type?' he asked with a raised eyebrow.

'Oh…nobody.' Chloe felt herself blushing. How the hell had he heard that in this throng of people? 'Steven, this is my friend and neighbour Gillian Denton. Gillian, this is my boss Steven Cavendish.'

'Pleased to meet you.' Steven smiled politely at Gillian and Chloe watched as her friend seemed to light up like a beacon.

'It's really nice to meet you.' She smiled.

Instead of leaving, Gillian continued to stay where she was as Steven sat down on the stool opposite.

Chloe noticed he was drinking a pint. It was strange to be out in a social environment with him. Although Chloe occasionally joined her fellow office workers for a drink, Steven rarely did…with the exception of the Christmas party and the intermittent leaving dos, he was usually winging his way home to Beth as soon as he could get away.

'So you're Chloe's boss.' Gillian leaned a bit closer.

'Yes, that's right.' Although Steven was being polite, he didn't really look very interested in Gill, which was unusual. Most men showed a lot of interest when Gillian was around.

'She's a wonderful girl,' Gillian gushed. 'One in a million.'

Steven looked over at Chloe and smiled as he noted the look of embarrassment on her face.

'Yes, I know,' he said to Gill.

'But sometimes too kind-hearted for her own good,' Gillian continued.

Chloe was starting to feel as if she wanted the ground to open up and swallow her. Was Gillian drunk?

Gillian met her eyes and winked. No, she wasn't drunk, just on a mission, Chloe realised, trying to think of something to say to make her shut up.

'Of course, Nile will be back once he realises his mistake…' Gillian continued, undeterred by Chloe's look of discomfiture.

Somewhere across the crowded bar, Gillian suddenly spotted her friend. 'Well, I'll go and let you two get on with your business meeting,' she said, giving a wave over at her friend. 'See you later, Chlo…nice meeting you, Steven.'

With a grin and thumbs-up to Chloe behind Steven's back, Gillian melted off into the crowds.

Chloe met the look of amusement in his eyes and cringed. 'Sorry about that… But she means well.'

'Who did you say she was?'

'My neighbour; she lives in the apartment across the hall.' Chloe sipped her wine. Considering the noise level in the pub, she was suddenly acutely aware that there was an awkward silence between them. What was she doing here? she wondered wildly. Her eyes collided with Steven's across the table and quickly skirted away from him again.

'So what did you want to say to me about the interviews tomorrow?' She tried to put the emphasis back on business.

'How many applicants have you got lined up?'

'Five.' She reached for her bag and searched through it to find the piece of paper that she had jotted notes on when she had phoned the agency that afternoon. She found it and smoothed out the creases so that she could read her writing. 'Four of them are English; one is from Scandinavia.'

Steven took a sip of his beer. 'What did they say about the one from Scandinavia?'

'Well-qualified…speaks good English.'

She glanced up and caught the gleam of humour in Steven's eyes. 'What's so funny?'

'Nothing.' He grinned. 'Well, actually, I was wondering more what she looked like...whether or not she was a Scandinavian blonde bombshell.'

'Oh, right; that matters, does it?' Chloe muttered, not in the slightest bit amused. 'Is that what you want me to put on my list of requirements—''Must be a gorgeous blonde bombshell''?'

Steven laughed. 'No, definitely not; I don't want any distractions on that front. Life is complicated enough. No, just find me a nice woman who seems trustworthy and kind and genuinely loves kids and I'll be happy...looks are not a requirement.'

Chloe nodded and took another sip of her wine. Some people sat down next to them; they were loud and full of boisterous high spirits.

'So what about hours?' Chloe said, trying to concentrate.

'I can't hear you.' Steven leaned closer across the table. 'What did you say?'

She leaned closer as well. 'I said, what about hours? Gina used to stay late during the week sometimes, didn't she?'

Steven didn't answer her straight away. He was looking at her as if studying her for a painting. Their faces were only inches apart across the table and as she looked directly into the darkness of his eyes she felt her heart speeding up.

'Where did you say you were going tonight?' he asked suddenly.

'I...I didn't say.'

'So...is it a date?'

Mindful of the fact that she wasn't going anywhere, Chloe pulled back. 'Why do you want to know?'

'No reason; I was just interested.'

'It's just...I'm meeting someone for supper, that's all.'

She felt herself blushing under his dark scrutiny. When he looked at her like that she felt sure he knew she was lying, felt sure he could look straight into her soul. Why was she lying? she wondered. What would happen if she said she wasn't doing anything this evening…? The temptation to come clean was almost overwhelming…but she didn't dare. It was better to keep barriers up where Steven Cavendish was concerned. He was her boss.

So why was he so interested in what she was doing this evening?

'Shall we get out of here?' Steven asked suddenly. 'I can't hear myself think.'

'OK.' Chloe finished her glass of wine and watched as Steven had a long swallow of his beer before leaving it.

'Whew I'm glad to be out of there!' he muttered as soon as they got out in the fresh air. 'It was stifling, wasn't it?'

'Yes.' Chloe had to agree, although she didn't know if it was the conversation with Steven that had been giving her warm flushes or the packed environment.

'How far is your flat from here?'

'Only about ten minutes.' She nodded towards a side road. 'Look, Steven, when you get home tonight, why don't you just jot down your requirements for a childminder—you know, hours et cetera; I can look at it in the morning before I begin the interviews. A bit like we did last time.'

Steven nodded. 'Yeah…OK.'

Why hadn't he just done that in the first place? Chloe looked at her watch, more for something to do than the fact she was at all interested in the time. 'Well, I may as well walk from here, seeing as it's such a nice evening.'

'I'll walk with you,' Steven said.

'There's no need.' She flicked him a puzzled glance.

'I know I don't need to…' He smiled. 'But I want to. Anyway, I could do with the exercise myself and, as you said, it's a nice evening.'

'Oh...OK.' She put her handbag firmly over her shoulder and stuck her hands in the pockets of her long trench coat. This was just getting weirder and weirder. She couldn't work it out at all.

Neither of them made any attempt to break the silence between them as they walked. It was as if they were both lost in their own private worlds. Chloe darted a couple of glances over at Steven, wondering what he was thinking about, and why he wanted to walk her home. But the handsome features were closed.

Maybe he was just glad to be out of the stuffiness of the office. Away from the main arteries, these back roads and gracefully elegant squares were quiet and peaceful and a gentle balm to the soul, especially at this time of the day.

They cut through another side road past mews cottages and then back out onto the square where Chloe had her flat.

As they approached the Georgian terrace Chloe started to cast about in her mind for something to say, something to put a close to the day and lessen the tension she felt inside. Nothing came to mind.

'Is Gina with Beth?' she asked finally.

'Yes; she's given four weeks' notice.' Abruptly he changed the subject. 'Do you think your friend was right when she said Nile will come back?'

They came to a standstill outside her front door. 'No, definitely not.'

'So you are not meeting Nile tonight, then?'

'No.' Chloe shook her head and searched hurriedly in her bag for her keys.

'Well, just as long as that caring heart of yours that your friend was commenting on doesn't overcome your better judgement.' His eyes moved with a kind of tender concern over her face. 'I wouldn't like him to get a second opportunity to hurt you—you're too nice, Chloe.'

'Am I?' Chloe's voice was light-hearted, but really she

wasn't too pleased with the analysis. 'Too nice' sounded sugary and without substance. 'Well, thanks for the vote of confidence,' she said lightly. 'But you don't really know me. For instance, I don't think I'm going to sign over my share of the house deposit to Nile until he pays some of these bills he's left.'

'I didn't know he had left you with bills.'

Chloe flushed. 'Well…he has,' she admitted. 'That was the main reason I asked you for that pay rise.'

'I see.' Steven's gaze seemed very serious suddenly. 'I assumed it was because you had been offered a better deal with your last company.'

She shook her head. 'No… Nile left things in a bit of a mess…' She trailed off, not wanting to even think about Nile. 'But I'm getting everything sorted out now.'

Steven had no doubt that Chloe was well able to handle the business side of her affairs. She was a capable and competent woman. But the hurt he had glimpsed in her eyes just now made him realise just how vulnerable she was feeling, and just how much of a betrayal she had felt at Nile's hands. 'Would you like me to sort things out for you?' he offered impulsively.

She looked slightly startled by the offer. 'No…thank you, but I can sort it out myself.'

Steven was aware that he was more than a bit disappointed by her reply. He would have liked to sort Nile out for a start…the guy sounded a real sharp character. The strength of his anger towards the other man astonished him. Maybe it was Chloe's gentleness or that vulnerability he had glimpsed for a moment in her eyes, but, whatever it was, he hadn't felt this protective towards a woman in years.

'Well, if you change your mind the offer stands,' he said casually. Steven reached over and took her front-door key from her. 'Have you got time to ask me in for a coffee?' he asked quietly.

The touch of his hands against hers sent a shiver of desire racing through her from nowhere.

The church clock from the far side of the square chimed the half-hour. Chloe's mind seemed to chime with them; in fact, alarm bells were racing through her entire system. 'Well...' She raised her face and looked at him. 'Just a quick coffee, then...because I don't want to be late for my supper date.'

'I won't outstay my welcome,' Steven promised.

CHAPTER SIX

STEVEN didn't sit down as Chloe went to make the coffee; instead he wandered restlessly around the lounge. He stood for a moment in the bay windows and looked out at the small park in the centre of the square. The sky was starting to turn a misty red as the daylight started to fade. One by one lights were flicking on in the houses around the square.

He turned his attention to the room. As he would have expected, it was very tidy. Vibrant tangerine settees contrasted with the pale walls and carpets. Candles lined the mantelpiece and also a few photographs. He went across to have a closer look.

'Who are the photographs of?' Steven asked as Chloe came back into the room with the coffee.

'The wedding photo is my dad and Margaret. One is my mother, taken on her twenty-first birthday.' Chloe went over to hand him the mug of coffee and glanced down at the photo he held in his hand. 'And that's my sister, Sinead.'

'She's a very attractive girl,' Steven commented, looking back at the photo again.

'Yes, very.' Chloe smiled. 'She is also extremely clever. She's training to be a doctor.'

He noticed how her voice was laced with pride.

'Are you close to your sister?'

'Yes; despite the age difference and, of course, the fact that we live so far apart now…we are still close.' Chloe perched on the window-sill and sipped her coffee.

Steven put the photograph down again. 'So, in spite of everything, you are really looking forward to her wedding.'

'Yes...'

There was a hesitation in Chloe's answer that Steven didn't miss.

'Who is she marrying?'

'Mark. He's a really nice guy and they seem very well-suited.'

'So what's wrong, then?' Steven leaned back against the fireplace and studied her intently from across the room. 'Why do I detect a hint of apprehension about attending the wedding?'

She frowned. 'I'm not apprehensive.'

'There's something wrong,' Steven said intuitively. 'Something that's putting you off going to your sister's wedding.'

'Nothing is putting me off going.' Chloe took a sip of her coffee and tried to ignore the silence, the way Steven was waiting for her to continue.

'You don't really want to go on your own, though...do you? Today, for instance, you were saying you might ask Cliff Roberts to go with you!'

'That was a joke.'

Steven looked at her with a raised eyebrow. 'But you don't want to go to this wedding on your own, do you?'

'Well, nobody likes to go to a wedding without a partner—it's one of those rare occasions when everyone seems to pair up, isn't it? Like Noah's ark.'

Steven smiled at the analogy. 'But there's more to it than that, isn't there?' he said gently.

She stared at him, her eyes narrowed. 'There's not much gets past you, is there?'

Steven shrugged.

'Well, if you really want to know—it's my dad. There is nothing he would like better than to see me getting married. And now that my relationship has broken down with

Nile he'll be lining up other suitable candidates for me to meet at the wedding.

'I know you're probably thinking, well, just ignore him and enjoy the day. But it's very hard to ignore Dad when he's on his soapbox. I just know he's going to try with his matchmaking schemes again. The last couple of phone calls I've had from him, he's been dropping hints about single men in the area. Things like, ''Did I tell you about Joe McCarthy, Chloe? He's got a smallholding of a hundred and twenty acres and all his own teeth.''''

'Well, as long as he wouldn't expect you to darn his socks.'

Chloe glanced over, caught his eye and smiled.

'Anyway,' she sighed. 'That's my dad for you. He's about as subtle as a brick through a plate-glass window. It's crazy, because these days a lot of women choose not to get married. Considering he's an intelligent man and a doctor, he's very old-fashioned.'

'He's just worried about you…that's a father's job.'

'Well, he needn't bother,' Chloe said crossly. 'I'm probably better off just concentrating on my career and forgetting about men completely.'

'Now that would be a terrible waste,' Steven said softly.

Something about the way he said that, the way he looked at her, made her temperature soar.

Steven put his coffee down on the table. The movement seemed so decisive that she thought for a moment he was going to leave, but instead he walked over towards her. 'I've had an idea,' he said.

'What kind of an idea?'

Steven leaned his hand on the window frame beside her head. His close proximity immediately made her acutely conscious of the effect he had on her. She noticed the way her heart rate increased, the nervous flutter in her stomach. She looked up at him and then wished she hadn't, as she immediately remembered how close he had stood to her on Friday night and the way he had kissed her.

Her eyes moved to his lips. No one had ever made her feel the way he had that night. It had been wildly and deliciously wonderful.

'How about if I accompany you to this wedding?'

'You?' She stared up at him in perplexity. 'Why would you want to do that?'

Steven shrugged. 'You bailed me out last weekend. I'd like to do the same for you.'

'But this isn't a trip down the road, Steven. It's a weekend in Ireland with all my family.'

'Sounds fun. I've never been to Ireland.'

'I don't know what to say…' Chloe was totally bemused by the offer. 'But…everyone will be expecting me to bring my boyfriend…and you are my boss…'

'Just because I'm your boss doesn't mean I can't be your lover as well. Or don't you think I could play the part in a convincing manner?'

The words seemed to trickle through her bloodstream, causing a riot of red-hot reactions… 'I don't know…why would you want to play the part?'

'I've got a number of dinner engagements myself over the next few months…and I've got no partner either,' he said easily.

'You mean it would be like a business arrangement?'

He could tell by the tone of her voice that the idea appealed to her. Steven shrugged. 'We don't need to write the terms down in stone, do we? I've stopped trying to plan life too precisely. Like the snow last weekend—you never really know what's around the corner.'

Chloe frowned. 'So what are you saying exactly?' she asked huskily.

'I'm saying that maybe we could be good for each other. You need a partner at this wedding. I've got a few engagements where I need a woman by my side... There's one dinner in particular next month. All the top management are coming to my house and I could do with a hostess.'

'Steven, I'm sure you would have no problem finding a woman to stand in as your partner. So why me?'

'Why not you? In fact, you are the obvious choice—you know more about the Cavendish business than any woman I know. You're intelligent, you're lovely, an asset to any dinner party.'

Chloe was silent for a long time as she tried to get her fuddled brain to work. 'The only drawback is that if you come to my sister's wedding and I start to act as your hostess at parties people are going to start thinking there is something going on between us,' she said edgily.

'Well, in the case of your sister's wedding, I thought that was the whole point.' Steven smiled. 'As for my parties, I don't care what people might think. As far as I'm concerned, you are acting as my hostess; it's no big deal. Neither of us is married...we won't be doing anything wrong.'

'And it would just be a straightforward, sensible arrangement that would suit us both,' she reiterated.

'Why do you keep emphasising that?' Steven asked tersely. 'Because I'm not your type?'

She remembered he'd overheard her saying that in the pub. The strange thing was, she hadn't really meant that; it was just something she had said to shut Gillian up. The truth of the matter was that she was starting to think he was very much her type. Maybe that was why she was so keen to emphasise the fact that anything between them would be strictly business...she was desperately trying to keep her feet on the ground where he was concerned. Desperately trying not to think about how much she wanted to kiss him again, fold into his arms. Because she knew he spelt danger. She knew instinctively that Steven Cavendish would have the power to hurt her if she let him…knew it because he made her lose control of her senses with such cool ease. And that was something that really frightened her.

'Maybe I'm not your type either, Steven,' she said, quietly now. 'That can work two ways.'

When Steven didn't answer her immediately she continued on, trying her best to be sensible. 'Plus, you are my boss. Crossing the line between work and social life could compromise our whole working relationship.'

'I'm willing to live dangerously if you are,' Steven drawled huskily. 'We kissed the other night and the world didn't stop revolving.'

He watched her face flood with colour and then smiled. 'And I think, judging by that kiss, we could play the part of lovers quite easily at the wedding party.'

'But we both agreed that kiss was just a moment of madness.' She felt quite breathless as he leaned closer.

He remembered the way she had kissed him on Friday night and felt a raw stirring of desire rise in him. A moment of madness it might have been, but it had been incredibly enjoyable. In fact, he hadn't been able to get it out of his mind ever since. Even in the office he couldn't concentrate on work for thinking about the heat of her lips, the curvaceous beauty of her body.

'Absolutely… A total moment of madness.' He leaned down even closer and took off her glasses. 'And I can feel another crazy moment approaching,' he whispered.

His lips were only inches from hers. She felt her heart thundering so hard against her chest that it felt as if it was trying to escape.

Then he kissed her. For a moment the kiss was questioning and hesitant, then as she responded it was fiercely possessive. Instinctively she slid her hands onto his shoulders as he pulled her up into his arms.

The daylight outside was fading, and maybe it was the semi-darkness of the room that emboldened Chloe, but one moment she was feeling uncertain and the next she was lost in the passion of his embrace and all she could think about was getting closer to him, having him caress her...make love to her.

He pulled away from her and looked at her, his dark eyes searching and intense.

Then, instead of either of them moving away from the situation, Steven gently led her to one side of the window and kissed her again, tasting her lips tenderly, then more forcefully as she responded with equal measures of passion.

She felt his hands moving to hold her, felt the heat of them burning through her clothes at her waist and her back. Then his fingers raked upwards into her hair, disturbing the clip that held it fastened so that it tumbled free around her shoulders. He tipped her head back, his lips moving to kiss the side of her face, then the side of her neck, sending waves of ecstasy shuddering through her entire body.

She felt his hands resting at her waist before moving upwards, stroking her breasts through the fine material of her blouse. Her body responded instantly to his caress, setting her on fire with a reckless desire.

The jacket of her suit dropped to the floor, and Steven started to unbutton her blouse. She knew she should say something to stop this, but she didn't want to. She wanted him, and that driving need was so forceful that it refused to listen to any small voice of reason. She stood very still as his hands pushed the material of her blouse to one side, then pulled at her bra to release the soft peaks of her breasts.

Her breath caught on a shudder of ecstasy as he touched her, his fingers gentle against her naked skin, exploring and arousing her with such ease that the thrills that shot through her were almost orgasmic.

Chloe's eyes closed on a wave of intense pleasure as he bent his head and kissed one rosy nipple.

As she felt his hand easing up her skirt and silkily stroking up over the lacy top of her stay-up stocking she tried desperately to gather some sensible words to stop what was happening, but her brain wouldn't function. *She didn't want him to stop.*

Her skirt slithered to the floor and she stood before him in lacy stockings and a very brief pair of string panties. He took hold of her hand and led her over towards the settee. Steven sat down and pulled her onto his lap, her knees at either side of his legs.

She stared down into the darkness of his eyes. 'We shouldn't be doing this.' Her voice was a husky, unsteady whisper. 'We've got to work together.'

'You're right,' he agreed huskily, but at the same time as he spoke he was easing her blouse down over her shoulder, kissing the naked flesh as he drew it off her to put it beside them on the settee. 'But for something so wrong... it sure as hell feels good.'

He reached behind her and unfastened her bra, throwing it down beside them as well. His thumbs stroked very gently over the curves of her breasts, and it was such sweet torment that she ached for the pressure to intensify, her breath sucking in on a gasp of sheer enjoyment as he reached and kissed where his fingers played.

Steven watched how she enjoyed his caresses, admired the pliant suppleness of her figure and the way her hair fell over her shoulders, gleaming silkily a burnished red with the reflection from the dying sun outside.

'This is so wrong,' she whispered, and yet at the same time she was reaching to kiss him on the lips, her mouth hungrily possessive and her hands unfastening his tie. 'But you're right, it does feel good.'

He detected a vulnerable need in her voice and it sharpened his desire even more.

He moved her slightly and unfastened his trousers.

Chloe was in the process of unfastening the first few buttons of his shirt when she felt him move against her.

'Aren't you going to get undressed…?' Her husky, shaky whisper made him smile.

'No time…' he murmured. 'Tell me that you want me,' he demanded gently. 'Say it.' His hand cupped her breast, his thumb rubbing over the sensitised peak until she moaned with ecstasy.

'I want you…' She couldn't think about what she was saying, what she was doing; it was as though some kind of fever had taken hold of her and all she could think of was appeasing the fire inside.

She sucked her breath in as she felt his fingers move to push the flimsy panties to one side, then gently stroking the soft wetness of her.

'You are a bit of an enigma, Chloe Brown,' he told her, his voice rasping with desire. 'Underneath all that straitlaced primness of yours there's a tiger hiding in the shadows. I think I always suspected it, but I was never sure until now…'

'Don't talk,' she murmured, her voice a pleading, shuddering whisper. 'Just take me…'

He entered the softness of her body, his body hard and demanding. His hands curved around her hips as he thrust against her, watching how she writhed with total abandon.

For a while he was able to control the wild need inside him and concentrate on pleasuring her, taking a voracious delight in the quiet gasps of her pleasure. Then, as her desire spiralled and threatened to get out of control, he allowed himself to join her in the blissful thrill of complete satisfaction.

When it was over she leaned against him, her body hot

against his clothing, her breathing ragged. They were both so out of breath that neither spoke for a moment.

He brushed the silkiness of her hair away from her face, which was buried against his chest.

She couldn't look at him; she was shaken and more than a little scared because she had wanted him so much. Allowing a man so much power over her emotions terrified her...she could feel panic welling up in her now as she realised how vulnerable she had made herself to him... She had cast aside her natural instincts of caution and reserve and that was something she had vowed never to do with any man. So much for trying to be sensible, she thought, feeling suddenly angry with herself, and then appalled by her complete lack of control.

Desperately she sought a way to backtrack, a way to find some kind of a safety net.

'So, what do you think?' Steven murmured playfully in the silence. 'We'd make quite a convincing act of being lovers, wouldn't you say?'

Chloe didn't know what to say. Her breathing was sharply uneven.

'Chloe?'

She looked up at him, her eyes wide and questioning. No man had ever made her lose her sanity like that before. What the hell had happened? she wondered dazedly. One moment they had been talking quite sensibly and then...whoosh! Emotional chaos.

'That's quite a chemistry that sizzles between us, isn't it?' Steven continued with a shake of his head.

'Yes...quite a chemistry,' she agreed shakily, and moved away from him, hurriedly reaching for her blouse, which was lying beside them on the settee. 'But it was just sex, of course.'

She was very grateful for the fact that the room was in total darkness now, the only light the soft glimmer of the electric street lamps from the road outside. Her fingers trembled as she fastened the buttons on her blouse. She was excruciatingly aware of how heavy the silence between them was now.

'Of course,' Steven muttered, feeling annoyed by the flippancy of her tone.

'Good.' She seemed to let her breath out in a sigh of relief. 'Well, as long as we both agree. I wouldn't want there to be any misunderstandings between us...that it meant more than it did. We've got to work together, after all. We don't want anything complicated.'

Steven reached to switch on the lamp next to him.

'No! Don't turn on the light!' Her voice was sharp with panic, which was in total contrast to the coolly dispassionate speech of a moment ago.

There was a second when he contemplated ignoring that plea and illuminating everything anyway.

'Please, Steven, leave it.'

The quiet anguish of her voice made him drop his hand. At least she wasn't as detached about what had happened as she was trying to pretend, he told himself.

She stepped into her skirt, but before she drew it up he could see the outline of her body against the window and he felt a new wave of desire rise in him from nowhere.

'Are you going to go now?' she asked quietly, zipping up her skirt.

'Do you want me to go?'

'Yes.'

He adjusted his clothing—not that much adjusting was necessary, she realised with another wave of mortified embarrassment.

Then he stood up and tried to reach for her, but she stepped back from him. 'Don't, Steven!'

'Why not?' he asked calmly.

'Because...' She was going to tell him that she was

frightened that what had just happened between them would happen again. 'Because you promised when I asked you in that you wouldn't outstay your welcome, and I want you to go.'

The tremble in her voice belied the steely tone of the words.

'Running late for your date, are you?' His voice was dry.

'Running very late…'

Steven smiled. 'We'll talk about this tomorrow, then.'

She was unprepared for the way Steven caught hold of her arm as he moved towards the door. Suddenly she was pulled close against him and he kissed her. She didn't want to kiss him back; she put her hand up to push him away, but there was no strength in her action, and her lips melted and responded to him as if by their own volition.

The shrill ring of the telephone was what made them pull apart.

'See you tomorrow,' Steven said, stepping past her towards the front door.

The phone continued to ring in the darkness of the room as Steven left, but Chloe made no effort to go and answer it.

She walked back to the window as the answer machine clicked in.

'Chloe, I thought we had a business agreement.'

She leaned her forehead against the coolness of the glass and watched Steven emerging out onto the street below.

'You said you'd think about signing the house over to me.' Nile's voice filled the air now, impatient and angry. 'Do you know how much money I stand to lose if you don't sign these papers?' Nile's voice rose even more. 'It's bloody ludicrous, Chloe; for a businesswoman, you haven't much sense.'

Now, that's the truest word you have ever spoken, Chloe thought wryly as she watched Steven walking away.

Chloe squeezed her eyes closed, trying to shut out Nile's words. This was how love ended, she thought bitterly.

And if she let Steven into her life it would be exactly the same... Wouldn't it?

'Can we meet and talk about this like adults? I'll ring you at work tomorrow.'

The line went dead.

CHAPTER SEVEN

CHLOE drew a line through the name of the third applicant on her list as the office door closed behind the woman. The interviews were not going well; there wasn't one person she had spoken to so far that she would like to leave in charge of Beth. And that was the last of the candidates for today. All she could hope for was that the women she would interview tomorrow would be better.

She flicked through her notes again and tried to ignore the fact that Steven had asked her to step into his office as soon as her morning appointments were finished. Chloe didn't feel she was ready to face Steven yet. Thankfully when she had arrived this morning he had been on the phone and there hadn't been a chance to speak about anything other than work. But the explosive nature of their situation had hit her as soon as she had looked at him and tension had seemed to be palpably hanging in the air.

There was a knock on her office door and David from the accounts department came in. 'Oh, good, you're still here.' He grinned at her, his boyishly attractive features lighting up as he saw her sitting at her desk.

'Of course I'm still here—it's only one-thirty.' She smiled back. 'When did I ever leave for lunch?'

'If you are looking for sympathy you won't get it from me,' David laughed. 'I keep telling you not to be so dedicated.' He perched on the side of her desk. 'So, how are things going?'

'Not so bad.' She leaned back in her chair and relaxed. She was used to David stopping and having a chat with her on the way through to Steven's office. He was a nice guy...probably about thirty-four, blond, not bad-looking in a studious kind of way.

Although it wasn't common knowledge in the office, Chloe knew he was seeing Cathy, one of the receptionists.

'What about you?' she asked.

'I've had better days.' He pulled a face. He nodded towards the inner office. 'What kind of mood is the boss in today?'

Chloe thought about that for a moment. 'I don't know; I haven't seen a lot of him. He's been shoulder-high in paperwork and I've been conducting interviews.'

'The work level here has been crazy, hasn't it? Let's hope this Renaldo deal goes through soon, before we all go nuts.'

'Amen to that,' Chloe said fervently.

'Listen, there's a bit of a celebration planned for Friday night and a few of us are going to the pub after work. Why don't you join us for a drink?'

'Yes, I'd love to come for a drink...' Her voice trailed off. 'Oh, wait a minute—I can't. I promised Steven I'd accompany him to Manchester on Friday. I've got to take some notes at another board meeting. I don't think we will be back until late.'

'Steven Cavendish takes up far too much of your time.'

That was what Nile had said before he stormed out, Chloe thought ironically.

David leaned closer across the desk. 'Tell him you've got friends who need you.'

'Maybe I'll be back in time to come—it's hard to say.' Chloe frowned. 'I'll ask Steven what time he thinks we will be back. I might be able to meet you later.'

Neither of them heard the office door open and they were both surprised by Steven's voice cutting across the conversation.

'You won't be back until about ten.' Steven supplied the

information drily. His dark gaze flicked from her to David, watching as the other man hurriedly straightened and stood up from her desk. He did not give the impression of being pleased. And the atmosphere in the office that had already been highly charged suddenly seemed to shoot off the scale.

What was he looking so irritated about? Chloe wondered. David had only been in the office for ten minutes. David darted her a look of empathy before picking up the papers he had left on her desk. 'I just brought up those figures you asked for,' he said, handing them over to Steven.

For a moment there was silence as Steven flicked over the pages. Then he glanced up. 'You haven't done the figures for the Galley Restaurant.'

'That's because I haven't received them myself yet.'

Steven frowned. 'Well, will you get them for me?'

'Sure thing.' David started to beat a hasty retreat towards the door. 'I'll have them tomorrow.'

'First thing,' Steven said drily.

'Yep…no problem.' With a smile in Chloe's direction David disappeared out the door.

Steven didn't move from the front of Chloe's desk, but continued to read David's report. It was a bit unnerving, having him stand there. She turned her attention towards her computer and tried to ignore his presence.

She wondered if he was regretting what had happened between them last night. The idea floated into her head from nowhere. Maybe he had looked at her this morning and thought, What the hell was I thinking of yesterday?

It was quite probable. It was what she had been reflecting on all night.

'How did the interviews go this morning?' Steven asked suddenly.

'Not too good, I'm afraid.' She took a deep breath and forced herself to smile up at him.

'I asked you to step into my office once you had finished.'

'Yes…I just haven't had a chance yet.'

He nodded. 'Well, will you step in now, please?'

'Yes, of course.'

He waited for her to precede him into his domain and then closed the door behind them.

'So, what did David want?' he asked tersely.

'He was just bringing you those figures,' Chloe said with a frown. 'Oh, and he was telling me that a few of the staff are meeting for a drink on Friday night.'

'Was that who you were supposed to be meeting last night for supper?' Steven asked suddenly.

'Who? David?' Chloe's eyes widened so much in surprise they almost rolled up through her head. 'Of course not! Are you joking?'

'No…just curious.' Steven sat down behind his desk.

There was a few seconds' silence, seconds where Chloe could feel her heart racing against her chest as his eyes moved over her contemplatively.

'We need to discuss what happened between us yesterday,' he said quietly.

'I don't think there is that much to discuss,' she said coolly. 'We had sex… I don't think we should let that fact ruin our working relationship.'

Steven's eyes held hers. 'Are you on the Pill?' he asked suddenly, and watched as her composure cracked slightly, a dull redness creeping up under the perfect velvet of her skin.

'You're a bit late asking me that now…aren't you?' she countered nervously. She didn't know what she had expected Steven to say to her this morning, but it hadn't been that.

'So, are you?' he asked again.

She pulled out the chair opposite him and sat down. 'Yes, I am.'

'Well, that's one less thing to worry about, then,' he said lightly.

'I didn't realise you were worried,' she grated sarcastically.

'I like to think I am a responsible male,' Steven said tersely. 'And, no matter what you might choose to think, I didn't go to your apartment last night with the express intention of making love to you.'

'I didn't think that for one minute,' she said heatedly.

'So why are you looking at me with such accusing eyes?'

'I'm not accusing you of anything.' She frowned.

She had spent last night going over what had happened in her mind, and if anything she realised that she had been the one to lose her restraint yesterday—she had almost begged him to make love to her. The knowledge was deeply shocking to her. She hated the fact that she had lost her control...that she had given herself to him so freely...so wantonly...it scared the hell out of her.

She needed to be in control; to open up to a man the way she had last night was a sure way of getting very badly hurt.

'I'm...I'm just angry with myself, that's all,' she admitted huskily. 'I liked our working relationship the way it was.'

'So did I, but I also liked what happened between us last night...in fact, I enjoyed it very much, and unless you are an exceptionally good actress I think you enjoyed it too.' He watched the discomfiture in her eyes. 'I meant what I said last night, about us hooking up socially—'

'And I meant it when I said crossing the line between work and social life could compromise our whole working relationship.' She cut across him sharply.

'I think we've crossed way over that line already, Chloe, don't you?'

His eyes flicked down over her figure. As usual she was wearing a smart business suit. It was a pale grey colour with a crisp white shirt beneath. He remembered the way he had undressed her last night, the surprise of finding such gorgeously sexy underwear and the womanly soft, sweet shape as she fitted easily to him. Suddenly he ached to reach out and start to unfasten those buttons, to caress and kiss the sweet flesh beneath.

'I think our relationship needs to go forward now, not back,' he said softly.

She felt his eyes on her body almost as if he was touching her, felt the immediate heat of desire sear through her from nowhere. Her heart slammed fiercely against her chest as she tried desperately to fight the sudden weakness invading every part of her.

'My offer to accompany you to your sister's wedding still stands,' he said firmly. For a second his eyes moved towards her lips.

'I've changed my mind about that idea,' she said shakily, annoyed by the way he was able to turn her on, just by looking at her. 'I don't think it's a good idea.'

'Well, I think it might be the perfect arrangement,' he continued in a businesslike tone. He reached across to the calendar on his desk. 'I've got that dinner on the twenty-sixth, which I could really do with you attending...and then there's the big bash at my house at the end of May with all the directors. Your help would be invaluable.'

The sudden switch from huskily seductive to purely business confused Chloe slightly. The way he'd worded that made it sound as if she was back in familiar territory.

'Look, Chloe, I realise Nile has hurt you, and maybe you are not ready to get involved with anyone else quite so soon. That suits me fine. In fact, better than fine; I don't want a heavy involvement myself.'

'No, I'm sure you don't,' Chloe agreed hastily. 'That was another reason why last night was a mistake…you've only just finished with Helen.'

'Absolutely.' He smiled. 'Last night was great. But I don't think we should let it ruin our working relationship…or come between us in any way.'

'Well, I agree with that,' she said cautiously.

'Great. Well, that's all fixed, then; you come to this dinner with me next Tuesday and I'll come to your sister's wedding. We'll be a great team.'

Chloe hesitated.

'It's a sensible arrangement, Chloe.'

His voice was so cool, so reasonable that she found herself nodding. 'Fine…as long as it's just dinner next Tuesday, Steven.' She forced herself to meet his eyes. 'I'm not going to sleep with you.'

'As I recall, we didn't do much sleeping.'

'You know what I mean.'

'Yes, I know what you mean.' He leaned back in his chair and shrugged. 'I've never forced myself on a woman in my life, Chloe; I don't intend to start now.'

'Just as long as we know where we stand.'

'Of course.' He smiled. 'Right, shall we get down to business? I need to send a memo to the office in the Isle of Man,' he continued matter-of-factly.

Hastily Chloe reached for a pen on the desk, the swift change towards business startling her.

'Mr James McCord, re advertising account…'

Steven usually dictated at a rapid pace, and today was no exception. Chloe's pen flew over the pad as she strove to keep up with him. Only when he paused for thought and to get his breath was Chloe able to glance up.

'Let's see…' Steven's eyes narrowed and he flexed his fingers as he thought.

Chloe's eyes moved over him pensively.

Had she done the right thing, agreeing to take him to Ireland? Last night she had told herself in no uncertain terms that if he mentioned accompanying her to Sinead's wedding again she would turn him down.

But why turn him down? Last night had happened; they couldn't undo it. It was just one of those things—a passionate interlude between two consenting adults. It didn't mean anything. In all honesty, she did think that Steven was probably still in love with Helen. He'd dated her for quite a long time. He might even have ended up marrying her if it hadn't been for the fact that Helen hadn't been particularly maternal towards his daughter.

Wanting a woman and yet having to give her up, knowing she was the wrong person for his daughter, would be hard for a man to reconcile himself with. It wasn't something he would get over easily…

Her eyes drank in the lean, handsome features.

He was a nice guy. She really respected the way he put his daughter first.

Why not bring him to Ireland? Everyone would be very impressed, and it would certainly shut her dad up for a while.

What was it Steven had said last night? 'I'm willing to live dangerously if you are.'

Well, why not? she thought. She had been trying to play her life in the safe lane for two years with Nile and look where that had brought her.

Steven continued with his dictation and she applied her concentration back to her work.

'You need to ring the Waterside this afternoon,' she reminded him briskly once he had finished. 'Oh, and the manager from the Galley needs you to run your eye over their new promotion.'

'Fine.' Steven checked his watch. 'I'll do it a bit later. What was wrong with the childminders you interviewed this morning?'

'Well…' She turned the pages on her notepad, looking for her observations from the interviews. 'The Scandinavian woman was very regimental; I think she would have had signs stuck up everywhere telling Beth not to do this and not to do that.' She glanced up at Steven. 'She was good-looking, however,' she added with a half-smile.

'That's her off the list, then,' Steven said with a glint of humour in his eyes.

For a second Chloe was transported back to the pub yesterday. She remembered the way Steven had looked at her across the table.

Quickly she continued reading from her notes. 'Then the second woman, Mrs McArthur—she was obsessed with manners and cleanliness…which is all very nice, but I think it was to the detriment of any real feeling. I think she would be happy as long as Beth was scrubbed up, but if she put a muddy footprint on the carpet, God help her.'

'So what about the third woman, then?'

'Mrs Reardon; she was a nice woman, but unfortunately she has six children of her own, and although they're all teenagers it means she definitely couldn't stay after seven in the evening.' Chloe glanced up at him. 'She was a good cook, however, and seemed a warm personality.'

There was a long silence while Steven digested all of this.

'I've got two more interviews tomorrow, so maybe we'll be luckier with them.'

'Maybe *we* will.' Steven smiled.

Chloe returned her attention to the dictation she had been

taking. 'Do you want to send this memo to the Isle of Man today?'

'Yep, soon as possible.'

The phone rang on his desk and he snapped it up.

'I'll get on with it, then.' Chloe got up.

'Fine; thanks.' Steven sounded distracted, his mind fully on whoever was on the other end of the phone.

She had worried too much about what had happened between them last night, Chloe thought as she went back to her own office and closed the door. Steven was too much of a businessman to let a moment of passion ruin their relationship in the office. It looked as if everything was going to be all right, and apart from the odd business dinner things would just carry on as normal.

Chloe sat back at her computer, trying to ignore the niggling voice at the back of her mind that was asking her why she had lied to Steven about being on the Pill.

CHAPTER EIGHT

CHLOE sat on a bench in the park and unwrapped her sandwiches. The smell of tuna was nauseating. Why hadn't she noticed that the fish was off when she had opened the tin this morning? Irritated, she quickly wrapped up her lunch again and got up to toss it in a waste-paper bin.

There wasn't time now to go and buy herself something else; Nile would be here in a minute and she had to be back in the office in half an hour. With a sigh she went and sat back on the bench.

She lifted her face up to the watery sun, thinking how pretty everything in the park looked. The cherry trees had suddenly burst into flower and tulips waved their heavy heads in the slight breeze that cut across the man-made lake. Hard to believe that only two weeks ago everything had been covered in a thick blanket of snow.

According to her watch, Nile was five minutes late. She wondered if she should wait for him, or if she should get back to the office early. Everything was in pandemonium back there, and had been for two weeks, because Renaldo had almost reneged on the takeover deal.

Steven had been stretched to the limit with it all; she had never seen him quite so tense. The only good thing to be said about it was that their…encounter at her apartment had been forgotten, swept aside under much more pressing concerns. Well, Steven had forgotten about it, at any rate, Chloe corrected herself. Unfortunately it did still creep into her subconscious from time to time. When his hand accidentally brushed against hers, when their eyes met in the few quiet moments between people rushing in and out of the office.

She had acted as his hostess for the first time last week. It had been an enjoyable evening: a relaxed oasis in the midst of what had been otherwise a turbulent week work-wise.

One of Steven's restaurants had supplied the food and they had sat in the formal dining room at his house with about six other people, all business associates. Because Chloe was so clued up with the business, conversation hadn't been a problem. And Steven had been the perfect gentleman, driving her home afterwards.

The only awkward moment had been when she was saying goodnight. She had suddenly found herself wanting him to kiss her. There had been a second when she had thought he was going to but he had simply seen her safely up to her front door, smiled, said goodnight, and turned on his heel.

The depth of her disappointment had stunned her. Wasn't that how she had wanted things to be between them?

A shadow fell across her and she glanced up into Nile's eyes.

'Hi, Chloe; sorry I'm late. I got held up at work.'

'That's OK,' she said easily.

He sat down next to her. 'So, how are things with you?'

'Fine, and you?' Her eyes flicked over him. Pleasant-looking, was how she would describe Nile; she had always liked his eyes, had always thought them kind and gentle.

'Oh, things are fine with me too.' He shrugged and reached into the inside pocket of his jacket. For a moment she wondered if he had remembered it was her birthday today and had brought her a card. When he brought out the papers that he wanted her to sign she almost laughed aloud at her foolishness.

Of course Nile wouldn't remember her birthday—it had

taken him all his time to remember it when they were together.

'It's good of you to sign the house over to me, Chloe. I
really appreciate it.'

Chloe took the papers and flicked through them.

'You don't need to read them,' he said in surprise.

She looked up at him briefly. 'Thanks for the advice, but
I never sign anything without reading it,' she said softly.

'Well, I've got to be back at work in ten minutes.'

She ignored him and continued reading.

Then, after a long silence while she concentrated, she
held out her hand. 'Have you got a pen?'

Hastily he scrabbled about in his pockets and brought
one out.

He watched as she signed on the dotted line.

'This is really good of you, Chloe; I really appreciate it,'
he said gruffly. 'And don't worry, I will pay you back that
money I owe you.'

Chloe was enough of a realist to suspect that would never
happen. But she handed him back the papers anyway.
'Have a nice life, Nile,' she said with a bright smile.

'Yeah…yeah, you too,' he said hurriedly as she got up
to go.

'Where have you been?' Steven asked immediately she entered the office.

'I just had a bit of business to attend to.' She hung her
coat up on the rail behind the door.

'You mean you were seeing Nile Flynn.'

She looked up at him, surprised by his observation. 'How
did you know?'

'He rang here, hoping to catch you because he said he
was running late,' he grated drily.

'Well, if you knew where I was, why bother to ask?' she
snapped in annoyance.

'Hey.' Steven perched on the edge of her desk as she sat down. 'Don't get grouchy with me,' he warned. 'Old age is no excuse for bad manners.'

'Old age?' She looked up at him through narrowed eyes.

'A little birdie on the window ledge informed me that it is your thirtieth birthday today.'

'Really?' Chloe pulled a face. 'I'll have that birdie for slander.'

Steven reached into the inside pocket of his jacket and brought out a small gift-wrapped box. 'Happy birthday,' he said.

She stared down at the box in surprise.

'It's safe to open,' Steven said with a glimmer of amusement in his eyes when she made no move to touch it. 'It's not booby-trapped or anything.'

'I'm very touched that you've remembered my birthday, Steven,' she murmured, still not reaching to open it.

Steven shrugged. 'I remembered your birthday last year, didn't I?'

She remembered the beautiful bouquet of flowers he'd had sent to the office and smiled. 'Yes, you did.'

'And, anyway, your birthday is only a week after Beth's, so it's hard to forget. She says thank you very much for her doll, by the way...she loved it.'

'Oh, I'm glad.' Chloe reached for the package. 'You know, you really shouldn't have done this.'

'I know, but I wanted to.'

He watched as she tore the paper away from the box and opened it. A delicate diamond cross on the end of a gold chain sparkled invitingly under the office lights.

'It's beautiful, Steven. Thank you so much.'

'Oh, and there's this as well.' He pushed a card across to her that had been lying unnoticed against her diary.

She tore it open, admiring the pretty picture of roses. All it said was a simple 'Happy Birthday', but beneath it was written, 'Love from Steven and Beth'. She noticed that Beth had written her own name and had put hugs and kisses next to it, and for some reason this really touched her. She felt her eyes mist over and blinked furiously, trying to pull herself together so that she could look up and thank him again.

'Don't be too upset—being thirty isn't that bad,' Steven said gently. 'In fact, they say life begins at thirty.'

'That's forty,' she corrected automatically.

'Is it? Well, never mind. Look on thirty as the starting block for happiness, then.'

She laughed shakily. 'You know, you really are quite poetic sometimes.'

'Do you want me to put that on for you?' he asked as she looked at the necklace again.

'Model it, you mean?' She looked up at him with laughter in her eyes now. 'I don't think it would suit you, Stevie.'

He stared at her for a second. 'No one has called me Stevie in years,' he murmured.

She felt her face redden; she hadn't even realised that she had playfully shortened his name. 'I'm sorry…'

'No, it's OK. Some wild woman used to whisper it in my ear as she asked me to make love to her, as I recall.' He watched her face go an even deeper shade of red and then grinned. 'That will teach you to tease me, Chloe Brown,' he said huskily, and then, getting up, he took the box from her hands and went around behind her desk to put the necklace on for her.

The touch of his hands against her neck sent prickles of awareness shooting through her along with a forceful need that sent her stomach into a kind of freefall.

'So, what are you doing tonight?' he asked.

She wondered if it was her imagination or whether his fingers were lingering longer than necessary against the sensitivity of her skin.

'Gillian wanted me to go out with her and a few of the other girls for a pizza, but I've put it off until next week because we're going to Ireland tomorrow afternoon and I need to pack tonight.'

'Packing on your birthday?' Steven sounded disgusted.

'Yes, well, it's been so hectic in here, Steven, that I've not had a chance to think about it until now.'

'Tell you what, take tomorrow morning off to do your packing and come out to dinner with me tonight. You were going to take Friday off anyway.'

'That was before we got so busy.'

'Chloe, I'll manage without you tomorrow morning. I'm only coming in for half a day anyway.' He bent his head so that his warm breath tickled against her ear. 'Don't tell anyone else that I've said this,' he whispered, 'but you can be too conscientious, you know.'

At the same time as laughing she was aware that she wanted to turn her head and kiss him. His lips were so close and she remembered how wonderful they felt against hers with a sweet, searing ache of need.

'I'd love to have dinner with you, Steven,' she whispered.

'Great.' He pulled away from her briskly. 'I'll pick you up at eight.'

She put on a pale blue dress that hugged her figure in a flattering way and then on impulse left her hair loose and put in her contact lenses.

She was just stepping back to assess herself in the bedroom mirror when the front doorbell rang.

Chloe pressed the intercom. 'Hi, it's me.' Steven's voice caused that fluttery sensation in her stomach that she was starting to associate with him.

She pushed the button to let him in and then stood with her lounge door open, waiting for him to come up the stairs.

'You're early,' she said as he appeared at the top of the stairwell.

'Yes, it didn't take me as long to get here as I thought it would,' he said with a grin. 'The traffic was very light.' His eyes flicked over her, taking in her appearance in one swift appraisal. 'Wow! You look lovely,' he said.

'Thank you.'

He looked sensational as well, she thought. His dark blue suit looked as if it had been styled by an Italian designer. Or maybe it was just Steven that made the suit look that good. He had that kind of continental flair of being able to make whatever he threw on look as if it had a designer label.

'Are you ready?' he asked. 'It's just that I left the car on double yellow lines; I thought it would save you getting wet if I parked straight outside the door. It's throwing it down out there.'

'I'll just get my bag and coat.'

Steven put his arm lightly at her back as they left the house together. The very lightness of that touch seemed to stir up her temperature, make her even more aware of the power he seemed to exert over her senses.

There was a wild part of her that wanted to say to him, Let's just forget about dinner; let's just stay in and we can make love. The need devoured her in a most disconcerting way.

She told herself fiercely to ignore it, that she was better sticking to this friendship angle…at least for a little while longer, to see how things went. After all, it wasn't long since he'd finished with Helen.

She remembered the red roses that Steven had ordered for Helen just days before they had split up. He'd had them delivered to his house so that he could give them to her personally. Although to her knowledge the order had never been cancelled, there had been no sign of red roses at

Steven's house when she had been there at that business dinner last week.

Chloe told herself that he had probably given them to his mother or one of his sisters, or maybe he had even thrown them in the bin. But there was a small part of her that wondered about that.

Maybe he had still given Helen those red roses.

She looked out at the dark wetness of the London streets and tried not to care about what he'd done with the flowers. It was none of her business anyway.

Steven looked across at her, a quizzical look on the handsome face now. 'Everything OK?'

'Yes…fine.'

'You're very quiet.'

'I was just thinking about what I'm going to pack into my suitcase tomorrow,' she lied.

'Beth has been packed for days,' Steven said with a laugh. 'Did I tell you?'

'No.'

'Oh, yes, she put the doll you gave her in, and a couple of teddy bears, and her favourite storybook. Plus four pairs of shoes and her favourite dress.'

'Four pairs of shoes!' Chloe laughed. 'She's a woman after my own heart.'

Steven laughed with her. 'Gina had a major job trying to persuade her to let her re-pack.'

'It sounds like she is excited about the trip.'

'I think that's an understatement.' Steven grinned. 'She's told everyone that she is going to your house in Ireland— even the cat next door.'

Chloe laughed. 'I'm glad she's looking forward to it.'

'It was kind of you to suggest I bring her along with us, Chloe,' he said softly.

'Well, there's loads of room at home, and my cousin's children will be there—Ellie has two little girls about the same age as Beth. Sarah is a bit older and Jane a year younger. They are going to be flower girls at the wedding.'

'It was still kind of you to invite Beth,' Steven said quietly.

'Who is babysitting for her tonight, by the way?' Chloe asked, changing the subject.

'Gina, although I had to beg and bribe her into it. I'm going to have to interview those ladies you put on your short list next week and make a decision on childcare.'

'It's a difficult decision.'

'Yes, it is. But you've helped a lot, Chloe.' He slanted a look at her that made butterflies dance in her stomach. 'Thank you,' he said softly.

'You know I'd do anything to help out where Beth is concerned. She is a wonderful little girl.'

Steven was gazing at her and he seemed to be deep in thought.

'You know, you and I should really be going out to dinner together on a regular basis,' he said after a moment. 'After all, we are in the restaurant business. We should be researching a different place to eat every week. It should come within the job description.'

'I'm glad it doesn't,' Chloe said fervently.

'Why not?'

'My figure would never recover.'

'I don't think you need worry about that,' he said huskily. 'Just for the record, I think you have a fabulous figure.'

For a second the image of his hands caressing her body flared in her mind, sending heat spiralling through her.

'By the way, I booked a table at the Waterside,' he continued briskly. 'I hope that's OK with you?'

'As it's probably the best restaurant in London, I suppose it will do,' she said flippantly. 'But if you want to do research, shouldn't we be trying out one of our competitors' restaurants?'

'You're probably right.' He glanced across at her again, a gleam of flirtatious humour in his dark eyes. 'But I wanted to do a different kind of research tonight,' he said in a low, seductive tone.

'A kind of quality-control check?' she joked lightly, and hoped she wasn't blushing.

'Something along those lines,' he grinned.

The Waterside was so named because it overlooked the River Thames. It was a modern building, the front a complete semicircle in glass so that each of the tables had a fabulous view of the river. The interior was a stylish mix of wooden floors and wrought-iron furniture, and built on three levels: downstairs there was the bar area that spilled out onto a terrace; upstairs there was the restaurant on two floors, linked by a black spiral staircase.

Chloe was extremely glad that she had worn her blue dress. It was stylishly understated, and in the fashionable surroundings of the Waterside she didn't feel too out of place.

The manager of the establishment, Jamie McDonald, greeted them warmly at the door and someone took Chloe's coat before they were led to the bar.

Although Chloe had been in the restaurant several times on work-related trips, she had never eaten in here with Steven. She sat on one of the high bar stools and sipped the glass of Chardonnay she had requested, and watched how the staff danced attendance around him, listened as Jamie talked business to him.

Usually she would have been interested in the business discussion, but tonight her brain refused to tune into it. Instead she was wondering what it would be like to have a full-blown affair with Steven Cavendish. Would it really be so unwise? Maybe after the emotional bruising she had received from Nile an affair was just what she needed, a frivolous, light-hearted bit of fun.

She studied Steven's profile as he talked. Then remembered the smouldering passion in his kisses and felt her stomach turn over with desire.

If Nile could bruise me, this man could devastate me, she thought suddenly.

Steven glanced across, caught her eye and smiled.

'Jamie, I think we will take a table and eat now, if you don't mind?' Steven cut across the other man as he started to talk about projected growth and advertising.

Immediately Jamie threw his hands up in the air, apologising for detaining them from their meal. He led them upstairs to a quiet table in the corner, handed them both a menu and discreetly left them.

'Maybe coming here wasn't such a good idea,' Steven murmured. 'We don't seem to be able to escape the spectre of work, do we?'

'It's no big deal,' she said lightly. Words that were in total contrast to the feeling inside that she would just like the whole world to disappear for at least an hour so she could have Steven to herself.

'You must be starving,' Steven said, opening the menu.

Actually Chloe didn't feel hungry at all. Her appetite seemed to have vanished, replaced by cravings of a much more perturbing nature, which seemed to strike every time he looked at her with that dark, intent gaze. 'I'm not too bad, really,' she said nonchalantly, transferring her attention to the menu.

For a moment there was silence between them, filled by the quiet buzz of the restaurant as it started to get busier. Chloe was acutely conscious of the fact that Steven was watching her from across the table. She wondered what he was thinking about.

'What did Nile have to say to you today?' he asked her suddenly.

She put down the menu. 'Not a lot, I signed his papers, so that made him happy.'

'Did he pay you the money he owes you?'

'Let's not talk about Nile,' Chloe said uncomfortably.

Steven shook his head. 'You should have let me deal with him for you. You're too soft...too vulnerable where he's concerned.'

'I just wanted closure on the past, Steven. I don't regret signing those papers, and in all honesty I wish him well for the future.'

Steven stared at her. 'Are you still in love with him?'

The quietly asked question confused her senses. 'No...not at all.'

Steven smiled. 'It was a silly question to ask you really.'

'Was it?'

He nodded. 'No matter how you were feeling inside, you'd still say no. You don't like to admit to any emotional weakness at all, do you, Chloe?'

She felt her heart thumping against her chest as she met his eyes.

'I'm right, aren't I?' Steven pressed.

'I don't know what you are talking about,' she said airily. 'You asked me a question and I gave you an honest answer...'

The waiter arrived at that moment to take their order. Chloe stared down at the menu without seeing anything and just ordered the first thing off each list.

Steven was right—she didn't like to admit to any emotional weakness...and why the hell should she? she asked herself furiously. It was better not to get emotionally involved at all. Opening up your heart to someone was tantamount to handing out a big sledgehammer and telling whomever you'd given it to to do his worst.

'I've hit a nerve, haven't I?' Steven asked softly once they were left alone again.

'No.' She held his gaze. 'I'm not in love with Nile; I'm not in love with anyone. In fact, I think I told you when I was at your house that weekend...I don't really believe in love at all.'

A waiter brought a bottle of champagne to the table and poured them both a glass before placing the bottle in an ice bucket next to them and leaving them.

'Happy birthday,' Steven said as he raised his glass towards hers.

After a moment's hesitation she joined him in the toast. 'Thank you.'

'I'm sorry if I was prying,' he said lightly.

She shook her head. 'No, I'm sorry to be so edgy. Maybe we shouldn't talk about Nile.'

'Or any kind of emotional involvement?'

She looked over at him questioningly.

'So, who is it that hurt you, Chloe...was it Nile or someone else?' he asked softly.

Suddenly her eyes seemed an impossible shade of violet-blue. 'When you said you wanted to do some research tonight I didn't realise that it was going to be quite so in-depth,' she said coolly.

Steven noticed the way her hand wasn't entirely steady as she picked up her glass and took a long sip.

'Well, as I'm going to stay with your family this weekend, I felt I should know a little more about you,' he said casually.

'There's not much to know.' She paused slightly before continuing to speak. 'Maybe I'm a bit raw from what's happened between Nile and me, but that's about all.'

Steven wondered why he didn't believe her.

Someone had hurt her very badly, so badly that she

found it hard to trust. He could see it in the wariness of her eyes.

Steven remembered that night at her apartment when she had given herself to him so freely and felt a surge of desire rising from nowhere. He wanted her again, had done for weeks. But he sensed if he wanted to get close to her on any level he would have to exercise a lot of control. However, that didn't mean backing down from something he knew was the truth.

'If you don't want to talk about it, that's OK,' he said gently. 'I can understand that. I didn't want to talk much after I lost Stephanie, not on any kind of deep level anyway.' He grinned, a kind of self-deprecating grin that made Chloe's heart squeeze painfully.

Then swiftly Steven changed the subject. 'So, tell me a bit about your family,' he said. 'Fill me in on details I need to know for this weekend.'

She felt herself relax as the focus of the conversation drifted away from her.

'Well, Dad is a family doctor, and Margaret, my step-mum, was his receptionist.'

'They met at work?'

Chloe nodded.

Steven listened as Chloe talked, noted the warmth in her eyes and in her voice. Obviously she loved her family very much.

'What about your family?' she asked him suddenly.

'My dad died five years ago. My mum took it hard—they were happily married for forty years.'

'Being happily married for forty years is a big achievement,' Chloe said softly. 'They were lucky to have that.'

'Yes, they were.' Steven's eyes moved thoughtfully over her face.

'And how many brothers and sisters have you got?'

'I'm the only boy and I've got five sisters.'

Chloe laughed. 'It's no wonder you are so at ease around women.'

'Oh, yes,' Steven grinned. 'I'm well-used to tights drying in the bathroom and razors that mysteriously go blunt. And I could probably tell you a fair bit about the art of co-ordinating your wardrobe as well.'

Chloe laughed. 'So where are your sisters now?'

'They all live away. Two are in America, one in France, one over in Holland. Maddi is the only one who lives anywhere near by; she's in Cornwall, which means she comes up for a visit more often than the rest.'

'Is she the one whose jeans I squeezed into?'

'Yes.'

'I must give those back to you. I've washed and ironed them but I keep forgetting to bring them into work.'

'There's no hurry.' Steven leaned over and refilled her glass. 'Tell me more about growing up in Ireland,' he invited lazily.

The time seemed to fly by after that. They talked about everything, and nothing, Steven drawing her out skilfully so that she found herself telling him things from long ago in her past, light-hearted, silly things she had almost forgotten herself.

When the waiter arrived at the table with their coffee she was aware of a feeling of disappointment that the evening was coming to a close. She couldn't remember a time when she had been so relaxed, so at ease in a man's company.

'Thank you; that was a lovely meal, Steven,' she said quietly.

'Yes, not bad.' He smiled. 'And the company was excellent. Do you know, I think this is the first time since that weekend we got snowed in that we've spent so much time in each other's company without mentioning work once?'

'Yes, I suppose it is.'

'And it's been fun.' His eyes held hers. They were dark and serious and they made her feel as if she was melting inside.

'Yes. It has.'

'Come on, I'd better take you home.' Steven lowered his voice conspiratorially. 'Let's escape before Jamie McDonald wants us to fill in a report card on the meal.'

After the jovial atmosphere in the restaurant, the journey back to Chloe's apartment seemed strangely silent.

Chloe's mind was running ahead, wondering if she should invite him in. She wanted to so much. Wanted to feel his hands against her skin again. Wanted to taste his kisses.

'Would you like to come in for a coffee?' she asked, somehow managing to inject a bright tone into her voice as he pulled into the square and to a standstill outside her apartment.

He switched off the car engine and looked over at her. There was silence for a minute, broken only by the sound of the rain drumming against the car. It seemed to fill the space between them like the drumming of her heart.

'No. I won't come in tonight, Chloe. But thank you for asking.'

'Oh, OK.'

'But I'll see you tomorrow. Pick you up at around one-thirty.'

She nodded, aware of a deep and completely illogical disappointment. 'Well, thank you again for a lovely evening.'

When he made no move to kiss her goodnight she leaned across to him and kissed him on the cheek.

The familiar tang of his aftershave sent a heady wave of feeling through her. As she moved to pull hastily back he stopped her by putting one hand on her arm. For a moment she looked up into his eyes and felt her heart thudding wildly. Then he lowered his head and kissed her. The touch of his lips against hers was electric; it filled her with such a need for him that she almost felt light-headed. His kiss started as gently persuasive and compelling and then as she kissed him back more hungrily his lips became harder, more demanding.

Then swiftly she pulled away and reached for the door handle of the car, running through the rain towards home.

CHAPTER NINE

CHLOE put the dishes from her lunch into the dishwasher. Then she glanced around the apartment, checking that everything was switched off.

Her suitcase stood in readiness by the front door, and everything was done. Any moment now Steven would be here. That thought brought a rush of excitement through her.

She walked to the windows and looked out.

The rain from last night had left everything looking fresh. The sky was a bright azure-blue, and a gentle breeze stirred the cherry blossom in the park, causing some of it to flutter to the ground like confetti.

She remembered the way Steven had kissed her last night. The masterful way his lips had aroused her, the sensation of need and ecstasy. If she didn't know herself better, she might imagine that she was in love with Steven Cavendish, she thought dreamily and then pulled herself up sharply.

Love didn't work; she didn't believe in it, she told herself staunchly. It clouded your brain so that you couldn't think straight and it ended in pain and disappointment. She was too sensible to fall in love with Steven.

So what were these feelings that assailed her every time he was near? she wondered. That weird feeling in the pit of her stomach as if her heart had slipped and bounced, that ache of longing when he touched her...

Steven's BMW turned the corner into the square. Hurriedly she moved from the window and checked her appearance in the mirror.

After much deliberation she had chosen the practicality of jeans and a lightweight top with a heavier matching jacket, because it was comfortable for travelling in. Her hair was neatly drawn back from her face and she was wearing a new pair of designer glasses that had cost her a small fortune. She probably shouldn't have bought them—she was only just getting back onto her feet financially—but they seemed to suit the shape of her face and she just hadn't been able to resist.

The shrill ring of the doorbell cut through her thoughts and hurriedly she pushed all of that to the back of her mind and went to let him in.

Steven looked summery and relaxed in a pair of fawn-coloured trousers and a lightweight shirt that seemed to emphasise the width of his shoulders and the perfect lines of his body. Gillian was right; he was gorgeous, Chloe thought as she stared into the darkness of his eyes.

'Hi. Are you ready?' He smiled at her.

'Yes, all ready,' she said breezily, and, trying to ignore those strange symptoms that were there again, she turned away from him and picked up her handbag.

'Is this all your luggage?' Steven asked, looking at her case.

She smiled at that. 'It's enough...don't you think?'

He grinned as he picked it up and felt the weight of it. 'There's nothing like travelling light,' he said.

'And this is nothing like travelling light.' They said the words in unison and then both laughed.

As the laughter died and their eyes met she felt the sudden surge of need rise in her again.

'Let's go, then,' she said, turning to lead the way downstairs.

Steven put her case in the BMW and Chloe transferred her attention to Beth, who was waving to her excitedly from the back seat of the car.

'Hi, darling,' she said as she slid into the front passenger seat. 'Are you looking forward to the flight?'

It was lucky that Beth was so talkative, Chloe thought as they made their way through the Friday-afternoon traffic towards Heathrow Airport. The child's constant happy chatter covered a tense silence that seemed to have descended between her and Steven.

She darted a sideways glance at him as they stopped for a moment at the traffic lights.

'It's warm, isn't it?' he remarked, and reached to switch on the air-conditioning. His arm brushed against hers as he moved and immediately she felt herself charged up with electrical current.

Maybe what she was feeling was an entirely physical attraction, she told herself sharply. Lust, that was what it was, a purely sexual attraction.

'Is that better?' he asked as cool air drifted over them.

She looked into his eyes and felt her stomach dip hungrily and her temperature soar. 'Yes, much better.'

No, it definitely wasn't love. Apart from anything else, the first rule of love had to be, don't fall for a man who will never return your feelings. That was just a one-way ticket to unhappiness.

Steven drove the car into the multi-storey car park and they took their luggage out of the back and headed for the lifts to the terminal. Beth clung tightly to Chloe's hand.

'Have you ever been on a plane before, Beth?' Chloe asked.

'Yes, Daddy took me to Disney World, but I don't remember it very much. I remember Mickey Mouse, though.'

Steven smiled. 'I'm not surprised you don't remember much about that journey; I think you were only four. It was just before you came to work for me, Chloe.'

As they mingled with the crowds to check in their luggage Chloe was suddenly picturing Steven alone at Disney with his daughter; he was a good father, she thought, caring and sweet and... She pulled herself up. He was also a man, and maybe he hadn't been on his own at Disney. Very probably he had taken a girlfriend as well. There had never been any shortage of girlfriends in Steven's life.

They picked up their boarding tickets and went through to the departure lounge.

'Would you like a coffee?' Steven asked. 'We've got about an hour to kill.'

'Yes, thanks,' Chloe smiled and brought Beth over to a seat in the window whilst Steven went to get the drinks.

Despite the fact that she had worked for Steven for a while, she didn't really know him that well, she told herself fiercely. Not well enough to think she was in love with him. They were relative strangers to each other really.

But Chloe wanted to know him. She wanted to know what he was thinking about when he looked at her, what made him happy, what made him tick...she wanted to know him inside and out.

She glanced up towards the coffee bar where Steven was waiting to be served, just in time to notice a very good-looking woman who was standing in the queue beside him smile provocatively at him. He smiled back at her, that easy, warm smile that was so attractive it was like a lethal weapon. The thrust of jealousy Chloe felt was quite out of proportion to anything that had happened or anything that was reasonable.

She glanced away, annoyed with herself. Then she added to the list of things she wanted to learn about Steven Cavendish... She wanted to learn how she could make him look at her like that, with sensual admiration in his dark eyes.

He came back to the table with their drinks. 'I bet you are excited to be going home,' he said as he met her eyes.

'Yes...very.'

Maybe tonight she should try to seduce him? The outrageous idea startled her; she had never intentionally set out to seduce a man before, but why not? She knew Steven wouldn't be averse to having sex with her, and maybe at the same time she would prove to herself that she wasn't in love with him. It was just sex, nothing more. She could take Steven Cavendish or leave him.

'What is your house like, Chloe?' Beth asked, interrupting her thoughts.

'It's big and it looks out over the sea and it's very pretty there. They say it's like an area in Italy called the Bay of Naples.'

Beth leaned her head in her hands as she listened intently. 'And are there really leprechauns in the garden?'

'Hundreds of them!' Chloe grinned. 'But you have to be quick to see them. They move very fast.'

'What shall I do if I see one?' Beth asked, her eyes wide with excitement.

'Catch him by the tail of his coat and ask him for a wish. You'll have to be specific, though…and polite… Leprechauns like good manners.'

Beth nodded. 'I'll try,' she said seriously.

Chloe looked back at Steven; he was watching her with serious eyes. Maybe he wasn't pleased that she was filling his daughter's head full of nonsense.

'I hope this weekend isn't going to be too boring for you, Steven,' she said.

He grinned suddenly. 'Don't be silly. In fact, as soon as we get there I might try to catch a few leprechauns myself. I could do with some help getting Renaldo to sign on the dotted line this afternoon.'

Chloe frowned. 'The takeover might go through this afternoon?'

He nodded. 'Yep…the contracts are due to be exchanged at four-thirty.'

'But it's scheduled for next Friday, not this Friday!'

'It was but they've brought it forward suddenly. I had a phone call at the office this morning.'

Chloe's eyes widened in horror. 'If that's the case you shouldn't be coming with me to Ireland, you should be at the office! This is really important, Steven!'

'Not more important than your sister's wedding, surely?' He smiled lazily. 'I'm a man of my word, Chloe, and a deal is a deal. I told you I'd come with you to Ireland and here I am.'

'But you could have cancelled your flight today and flown out tomorrow instead. The wedding isn't until to-morrow anyway... I'm just going early because I need to be there for a fitting for my bridesmaid dress tonight—'

'Chloe.' Steven cut across her firmly. 'I don't need to be there for the signing of the contracts. I've done all the pre-liminary work. It's down to the solicitors now.'

Chloe thought about this for a moment. She supposed he was right; the contracts did depend on the solicitors. Even so, she was touched that Steven hadn't wanted to let her down today; nobody had ever put her first like that before.

Their flight was announced at that moment and Steven smiled. 'Anyway, it's too late to change my mind now. We're on our way.'

Their flight touched down at Dublin Airport about an hour later, and it didn't take long to collect their luggage and their hire car.

It was warm and sunny, and as Steven stowed their bags in the back of the car Chloe took off her jacket, glad of her lightweight T-shirt beneath.

'That lady thought you were my mummy,' Beth told her as Chloe bent to help her take off a few of her outer clothes as well.

'Which lady, darling?' Chloe asked absently as she

handed Steven the coats so he could throw them in the back with the bags.

'The lady on the plane; she asked me if I wanted to sit between my mummy and daddy or by the window.'

'That was the air stewardess.' Chloe noticed that Beth's hair had escaped from its pony-tail and bent to fix it. 'And I guess it's an easy mistake for her to have made. I suppose we looked like a family.'

As she straightened she met Steven's eyes over the top of the child's head. He was looking at her in a very strange way; she couldn't quite fathom what he was thinking, and before she could even try he had turned away.

'Climb into the back of the car now, Beth, and put your seat belt on,' he said, closing the boot of the car.

'Do you know the way from here?' he asked as they all got into the white Mercedes. 'Or do we need that map the car-hire people gave us?'

She smiled. 'I'd know the way blindfolded, Steven.'

They didn't talk much as they negotiated the traffic. Chloe directed Steven so that he didn't have to drive through the centre of the city and instead headed out across the toll bridge.

The road hugged the coast for a while, and as Chloe looked out over the blue sea and the brightly coloured Georgian houses that looked across Dublin Bay there was a sudden feeling of happiness and nostalgia in her heart.

'I used to come to college this way,' she remarked. 'I took the Dart…that's the train. It follows this coast through some spectacular scenery.'

'Feel good to be back?' Steven asked, taking his eyes off the road to glance at her.

She nodded. 'It's strange, but I didn't realise just how much I had missed it until now.'

'How long is it since you were home?'

'Two years…just before I met Nile.'

'That's a long time. As it's such a short flight, I'm surprised you're not back and forwards every other weekend.'

'Well, you know what life is like. You're busy and time seems to pass so quickly.'

'I hope it's nothing to do with the fact that I've been working you too hard?'

She smiled and shook her head. 'I've seen my dad in that time. He came and stayed with me in London for a week last year.'

'Why did you move back to England anyway?' Steven asked curiously.

'I was offered a transfer with the company I worked for in Dublin to their London base. It was too good a career move to turn down. And I suppose I fancied being a bit more independent, spreading my wings a bit.'

'Is that the company who wanted to steal you away from me again?'

'Yes.' She couldn't resist adding light-heartedly, 'But I'm glad I didn't go back.'

'So am I,' Steven said softly. 'You turned my office around the day you walked in.'

'As long as I didn't turn it upside-down.'

'You're very good at your job, Chloe, as well you know. And I'd hate to lose you.' He caught her eye. 'In any capacity,' he added softly.

Was that his way of saying he liked this businesslike arrangement they had in their social life as well?

'So, what did you tell your father about me?' he asked, changing the subject.

'Not a lot.' She smiled. 'And please pay no attention to him when he starts with his usual it's-time-my-daughter-got-married routine. Do as I do and switch off to it. Rising to the bait and starting a discussion on it only makes him worse.'

'How serious do you want him to think we are about

each other?' Steven asked. 'What are the sleeping arrangements for the weekend?'

The nonchalant questions sent heat sweeping through her entire body. She looked over her shoulder at Beth.

'She's asleep,' Steven said, correctly interpreting what she was doing. 'So you can tell me all about it without fear of little ears.'

Chloe hesitated. 'I haven't led anyone to believe our relationship is serious. Margaret said she'd put Beth in a twin-bedded room next door to my double bedroom. So I suppose she is leaving it up to me how we choose to arrange things.' She glanced up at the road. 'You need to take the next turning right, by the way,' she added.

'And how were you planning on arranging things?' Steven asked.

The direct question unnerved her. She could hardly say, Well, actually I want you in my double bed...could she? She noted the lazy humour in Steven's eyes. Obviously he found the situation amusing. 'Well, either you can take the double bed, or I can,' she said awkwardly.

'We'll sort the details out later, then, shall we?' he said easily, and she almost sighed with relief.

'Yes...fine...whatever.'

He smiled. 'Whatever,' he agreed with a gleam of teasing warmth in his eyes.

In the ensuing silence some very strange thoughts flicked through Chloe's mind, mostly to do with how she could get Steven Cavendish into her bed. Maybe she could lure him in with a see-through negligee; trouble was, she had no see-through negligee. She smiled to herself, wondering quite suddenly if she had lost her sanity.

'Our house is just up there.' She pointed to a gateway almost obscured by greenery on the country lane.

Steven turned the car up the long drive that wound around the beautifully manicured gardens up the steep hill.

Now that she was almost home, Chloe started to feel a tad apprehensive about what she was about to do.

It was one thing sitting in at Steven's business dinners, but bringing him home to her family...planning to seduce him...was another!

CHAPTER TEN

AS THE car came to a halt the front door opened and Sinead ran out to greet them.

'You're here at last,' she said, flinging herself into Chloe's arms. 'I thought you were never going to arrive.'

Chloe hugged her sister tightly and it was a few minutes before the two women let go enough of each other for Chloe to introduce her to Steven.

'Hi, pleased to meet you.' Steven was going to shake hands, but Sinead reached up and kissed him on the cheek.

'It's lovely to meet you,' she said warmly. 'We've heard so much about you.'

'Have you?'

It was no wonder Steven looked a bit mystified by that statement—so did Chloe. She didn't think she had talked that much about Steven. The bare minimum was what she had told Sinead on the phone. Just that her relationship hadn't worked out with Nile and she had found herself drawn instead to her boss.

'All good, I hope?' Steven asked with a grin.

'Absolutely.'

'You look great, Sinead,' Chloe said, changing the subject. Her sister did indeed look very well. Her blonde hair was highlighted with pure golden streaks and her skin was perfect, as was her figure in the blue summer dress.

'So do you,' Sinead said. 'Obviously love is agreeing with you.'

Chloe caught Steven's eye and tried very hard not to blush. She was very thankful when her dad and stepmum came out of the house at that moment.

Chloe hugged them both, and then hugged her dad again. 'It's really good to see you, Dad,' she said, looking up into the gentleness of his blue eyes. 'You look well; a few more grey hairs maybe...' She tried to make a joke to hide the fact she felt suddenly emotional. The fact was, her father's hair had been pure white for as long as she could remember.

Graham Brown looked similarly moved as he held his daughter close. 'You've been away that long you've forgotten what your dear old dad looks like, that's your problem,' he scolded gently.

For a while they stood in the warm sunlight while Chloe made the introductions with Steven and they all chatted happily, asking the usual questions about the journey and the weather. Then suddenly she remembered Beth.

She turned towards the car and saw that the little girl was still fast asleep.

'Beth, honey?' Chloe opened the door and touched her shoulder gently. 'Beth, we're here.'

The child opened her eyes and seemed to be totally disorientated. Then she allowed Chloe to help her out of the car. She stood looking a trifle bewildered as everyone said hello to her, her blonde hair ruffled and her cheeks flushed from sleep. And as Margaret bent to ask her if she would like to come inside and have lemonade she buried her head shyly against Chloe's legs.

'You'd love some lemonade, wouldn't you, sweetheart?' Chloe lifted her up into her arms. 'Shall we go inside and see what else we can find for you...maybe some chocolate?'

'She'll be all right once she meets Sarah and Jane,' Sinead said. 'That's my cousin's children,' she told Steven. 'They are out in the back garden, playing; I don't think they heard the car.'

Steven watched how Beth clung to Chloe, wrapping her

arms around her neck and shooting shy glances out at everyone from big blue eyes. He noted the instinctive tenderness Chloe had with her, the way she stroked a stray strand of hair from Beth's eyes and smiled at her. And he felt something inside him squeeze tightly.

'Gosh, but you're heavy.' Chloe laughed over at Steven. 'I'm sure she's grown another few inches during that drive. If she keeps this up I soon won't be able to pick her up at all.'

'Do you want me to take her?' He moved to stand next to them.

'No, I'll manage. I'll leave you to bring in the bags.' Her eyes danced mischievously as they looked up at him.

'You haven't overdone the luggage again, have you, Sis?' Sinead laughed. 'Chloe never travels lightly; there's always an excess-baggage fee when she gets to the check-in, and that's when she's just brought an overnight case. You've got a lot to put up with, Steven.'

'Oh, I don't mind.' Steven smiled with lazy good humour into Chloe's eyes. 'Chloe's worth the trouble…and the torn ligaments.'

They all laughed.

'I'll give you a hand, Steven,' Graham offered as the women headed indoors.

The large house was just as Chloe had last seen it, its beautiful interior restored to the eighteenth-century grandeur of when it had been an old coaching house. The main hallway was flagged and led down to the downstairs drawing room with gracefully curved windows that looked out over the sloping gardens to the Irish Sea. A magnificent stained-glass window lit the enormous stairwell, the jewelled colours reflecting on the flags and the polished wood of the furniture.

The kitchen had always been the heart of the home and it seemed little had changed there either. The smell of baking filled the air and pots bubbled on the Aga, whilst the huge table was strewn with the calorific delights of Margaret's efforts.

'Heavens, Margaret, you look like you're expecting an army,' Chloe laughed, pinching a chocolate Wellington square and giving it to Beth.

'Graham thinks that if we go to the pub for a drink tonight a few people might come back.' Margaret grinned as she switched on the kettle. 'You know how it is.'

Chloe knew how it was indeed. 'Any excuse to begin partying,' she said with a laugh.

As Margaret tried to make them all a cup of tea she was interrupted time and again by the phone ringing. Chloe set Beth down in the chair by the fireplace and automatically set to helping as Margaret talked to everyone from the caterers to some friends who had rung for directions to the church on Saturday.

'I'm so glad you're here, Chloe,' Sinead said as she perched on the arm of Beth's chair. 'It's been like this for days now; we've hardly had time to turn around.'

'Planning a wedding is obviously a bit like planning a campaign of war.' Chloe smiled as she opened the fridge to get some milk and noticed the list of tasks for the wedding that Margaret had stuck on the front with a fridge magnet.

'Tell me about it!' Sinead rolled her eyes. 'And it's got crazier by the day. Mark and I are starting to wonder if we should have run away and just got married on a Caribbean beach.'

'Chloe, who is outside in the garden?' Beth asked, kneeling up on the chair to look out of the window.

'That's my cousin Ellie's children. Where is Ellie, anyway?' Chloe asked Sinead.

'Went into Dublin first thing this morning on a shopping spree and hasn't come back yet.'

Chloe put the teapot on the Aga to brew and as the phone continued to ring took Beth out to the back garden to say hello to Sarah and Jane.

'It doesn't take children long to overcome their shyness, does it?' Sinead laughed as a few minutes later all three children had disappeared down to the Wendy house at the bottom of the garden and were playing happily.

Chloe smiled as the contagious sound of the children's giggles drifted in the warm evening air.

'Steven is really attractive,' Sinead murmured. Turning, Chloe followed her sister's gaze towards the window, where she could see Steven and her father walking into the kitchen. 'It's no wonder you've had a thing for him for the last two years.'

'I haven't really had a…thing…for him for two years,' Chloe corrected as she returned her attention to her sister. 'It's fairly recent.'

'No, it's not. Every time you've ever mentioned Steven your voice has gone very mysterious. You've always liked him.'

Before Chloe had a chance to answer this Sinead continued hurriedly, 'Anyway, while I've got you on your own, Mum wants me to check the sleeping arrangements with you. We've put Steven in with you, of course, but do you think Beth will mind sharing with Sarah and Jane? It's just that Mark is short of a bedroom for one of his relatives and we thought he could stay here. If you wouldn't mind?'

Chloe opened her mouth and nothing came out for a moment. She wanted to be with Steven and maybe this was her perfect excuse.

'Is that all right, Chloe?' Sinead asked again with a frown. 'The girls are about the same age as Beth…and they do seem to be getting along very well together.'

Chloe knew she should say, Well, it's all right for Beth

to double up, but Steven and I need separate rooms. But instead she found herself saying, 'That's fine, Sinead.'

'Thank heavens for that.' Sinead let her breath out in a sigh of relief.

'Thank heavens for what?' Steven asked as he stepped out of the back door to join them.

Instantly Chloe's trepidation mounted. What on earth was Steven going to think when he heard that she had just agreed to them sharing a room?

'That you don't mind Beth sharing a bedroom with my cousin's little girls.' Sinead smiled.

'Of course not.' Steven glanced at Chloe, noting immediately the sense of unease about her.

'Usually space isn't a problem here,' Sinead said. 'But with this wedding coming up it feels like we need to have elastic walls.'

'Maybe we should have stayed in a hotel,' Chloe murmured. 'It might make things easier.'

'Are you joking? We want you here, Chloe.' Sinead looked horrified. 'Don't say that to Mum and Dad...whatever you do. They'd rather throw everyone out on the street than have you and Steven move out.'

'Sinead, Mark's on the phone,' Margaret called from the open doorway.

Sinead hastily excused herself and ran inside.

'Everything all right, Chloe?' Steven asked quietly once they were left alone.

'Well...' She looked up into the darkness of his eyes. 'We've got a slight problem with the sleeping arrangements,' she admitted huskily.

Steven smiled. 'Yes, so I gathered.'

Chloe felt her skin burning with embarrassment as his eyes travelled over her face searchingly.

'So it means we will be in the same bedroom.' She tried very hard to sound matter-of-fact about the prospect.

As the minutes ticked by and Steven didn't say anything Chloe felt her nerves twist and tingle all the way down to her toes.

'I suppose I could have a quiet word with Margaret and we could rearrange the rooms,' she said finally in desperation; she didn't want to force the situation. 'The children could share the double bed in my old bedroom and we could have the twin-bedded room...'

'If that's what you want to do...' Steven shrugged. 'But frankly I think you would be creating a big fuss for very little difference. We'd still be sharing a room.'

'So is that all right with you?' she asked hesitantly. 'Or would it be better if we moved to a hotel?'

'Chloe, I do have some self-control, you know. Just because we are sharing a double bed doesn't mean I'm going to automatically expect to have sex with you.' He smiled as he watched the heat rise again under the delicate creaminess of her skin. 'Hey.' He reached out and tipped her chin up so that she was forced to hold his direct dark gaze. 'I'd never hurt you, Chloe. You know that, don't you?'

The light touch of his fingers against her skin made her tremble inside.

'OK...so we won't make a big deal out of this and we'll just leave things as they are,' she said huskily.

Steven nodded. 'Good idea; I think Margaret has enough on her plate organising this wedding without worrying about where everyone is sleeping.'

'Chloe, we need to go down to the wedding boutique so that you can try your dress on,' Sinead called from the doorway. 'I think we should go now; I told them we would be there as soon as possible, because they're keeping the shop open a bit later for us.'

'Yes, of course.' Chloe looked up at Steven. 'I won't be long; why don't you ring the office while I'm gone...find out if Renaldo signed on the dotted line?'

'Do you know, I think you are more worried about that business than I am sometimes?' Steven grinned. 'And that's saying something!'

Chloe smiled. 'I'll see you later, then.'

'Yes, darling,' he murmured and, bending, he kissed her full on the lips. The movement was completely unexpected and for a moment she swayed against him, her lips instantly softening and responding to his.

'See you later.' He smiled at her as he pulled away, the throaty promise in his voice sending tingles of excitement through her.

It wasn't until she turned to go into the kitchen that she realised that Steven had probably only kissed her for the benefit of all her family, who were standing watching.

'I can't believe how good that dress looked on you,' Sinead said as they turned back into the driveway a few hours later. 'And it fitted you perfectly. I was so worried that it wouldn't! That maybe we had made a mistake with the measurements. But you looked incredible.'

'So did you. I love your wedding dress, Sinead. You're going to be the most beautiful bride.'

'Thanks, Chloe.' Sinead looked over at her sister. 'You know, I'm sorry things didn't work out for you with Nile. Are you really as all right about the break-up as you seem?'

'Yes; I think it was my pride that was hurt more than anything else. On reflection, it was a wise decision to split. We weren't suited...he did me a favour really.'

'Yes, because Steven is gorgeous.'

'Yes, he is,' Chloe agreed with a laugh. 'But don't go rushing to conclusions, Sinead—'

'I'm not,' Sinead cut across her. 'But, you know, I re-member ringing you up to ask how your first week at work went and you talked non-stop about him. There was this kind of spark in your voice that I'd never heard before. I was half expecting you to ring me back a week later and tell me you'd ditched Nile.'

Chloe shook her head. 'Sparks do fly between us, but it's mostly to do with work. You probably misunderstood.'

'I don't think so,' Sinead laughed. 'It's called chemistry, Sis, and you and Steven seem to have it in spades.'

Sinead brought the car to a full stop in front of the house. 'Now that's done, let's round up the men and go down to the pub for a drink. Don't worry about Beth, because Ellie has offered to babysit.'

'I'll have to check with Steven about that. He might not want to leave her. Not when she's just arrived and everything is a bit strange to her.' Chloe stepped out into the cool of the evening air and helped Sinead take the dresses out of the back of the car. 'Anyway, isn't it unlucky to see the groom on the night before the wedding?'

'If it is I don't care,' Sinead laughed. 'Now that I've tried my dress on again and seen you in yours I know nothing can go wrong.'

Steven and her father were in the lounge drinking coffee when they walked in.

'Hi; how's everything?' Chloe smiled at the two men, at the same time hoping her father hadn't been saying anything too embarrassing in her absence. 'Dad hasn't been showing you pictures of me when I was a baby or anything awful like that, has he?'

'Oh, yes, I've seen all your baby pictures,' Steven said. 'Even the ones of you naked in the bath.'

'Dad, you haven't!' She glared at her father, caught him laughing and realised Steven was teasing her. 'Very funny, Steven,' she said drily.

'How did the dress fittings go?' he asked with a smile.

'Perfectly,' Sinead gushed. 'Chloe looked sensational.'

'Chloe always looks sensational,' Steven said softly,

watching Chloe's discomfiture with a certain amount of pleasure.

'Yes, all right, Steven, don't overdo the compliments,' she said.

Chloe's eyes drifted over him, noting he had showered and changed. He was wearing a pair of black jeans and a sports top that made him look extremely sporty and handsome.

'So, what is the plan for this evening?' Sinead asked. 'Chloe says she can't come to the pub with us for a drink because she doesn't want to leave Beth.'

'Really?' Steven looked over at Chloe.

'I know Ellie said she would babysit,' Chloe said. 'But Beth might feel a bit insecure in unfamiliar surroundings, so—'

'I don't think that's going to be a problem, Chloe,' Steven cut across her. 'Beth is in her element with Sarah and Jane—in fact, she is happier than I've seen her in ages. Your cousin said she'd ring me on my mobile if there was a problem. And, anyway, apparently the pub is only down the road.'

'Great,' Sinead smiled. 'Hurry and get ready, Chloe; I'll go ring Mark and tell him we'll see him there.'

There was a woody smell from the turf fire burning in the stone grate beside them and it mingled pleasantly with the scent of Chloe's perfume as she leant across to introduce Steven to a few more of her friends who had just arrived.

The small inn was packed to capacity, and Steven wondered about the fact that it was now heading up to midnight, yet more people were arriving and the landlord was still serving.

'At home they'd have rung a bell and called time long ago,' Steven told Graham, who was sitting beside him.

'We're a bit more relaxed around these parts,' Graham answered with a smile.

Some music started up at the far end of the room and a few people who were standing beside them at the bar started to sing. Steven noted with amusement that Chloe was one of them.

'Chloe has a fabulous voice, you know.' Graham leaned closer. 'Have you heard her sing?'

'No, I didn't know she could.' Steven was watching Chloe with close attention. She was wearing a pale pink dress; the soft folds clung to her figure, emphasising its curvaceous beauty, and her skin glowed with a healthy peach vitality. He wondered if the contact lenses she wore were coloured, because her eyes seemed an even brighter shade of blue than usual.

He smiled as he watched her laugh as the song ended, her head tipped back slightly, her hair tumbling about her shoulders, flaxen in the half-light of the fire. She caught Steven's eye and smiled at him.

At one time she would have hurriedly looked away at this point, but she didn't tonight; she held his gaze in a way that turned his blood to fire. He wanted her so much... The thought of being alone with her in a double bed tonight sent a wave of impatient need through him.

He remembered what he had said to her this afternoon, about not taking advantage of the situation...being perfectly able to sleep next to her in a bed without wanting her...and the lie of it seemed to mock him with taunting cruelty. Who the hell had he been trying to kid?

'I can see that you are very taken by my daughter,' Graham said, distracting Steven's attention.

He tore his eyes away from Chloe. 'Who wouldn't be?' he said quietly. 'She is beautiful.'

'And happier and more relaxed than I have seen her in a long time,' Graham reflected.

'It will take her some time to get over Nile, I suppose.' Steven reached for his pint.

'Perhaps.' Graham thought about Steven's words for a minute, and then shook his head. 'She was very fond of Nile, but I don't think it was a particularly passionate relationship.'

'What makes you say that?' Graham had his full attention now.

'I spent a week with them in London.' Graham shook his head. 'Chloe thought she could fool me, but she couldn't. Nile wasn't deeply in love with Chloe and Chloe knew it right from the start. I suspect that's what she liked about the relationship—it wasn't all-consuming; in fact, it was more like a friendship than a love affair. She thought he wanted her for all the right reasons. He respected her, she said, he was as focussed on his career as she was on hers. She gave me all this blether about them going in the same direction, wanting the same things.' Graham shook his head. 'Did you ever meet Nile?'

'Yes, once, at the Christmas party. A very quiet guy, as I recall.'

'Ineffectual, is the word you are looking for,' Graham muttered. 'Couldn't light a fire under my daughter if you'd handed him a box of firecrackers. Spent all his time with his head in his books; ignored her a lot of the time.'

'Well, why would Chloe want to marry someone like that?' Steven was stunned.

'I think she saw him as solid and reliable. She's been badly hurt in the past, Steven, and she has experienced and seen some dreadful things.'

'What kinds of things?'

'Has she ever talked to you about her stepfather?'

'No.' Steven frowned. 'I didn't know she had a stepfather.'

'That doesn't surprise me, somehow. It's something

Chloe wants to forget. I shouldn't have mentioned it.'
Graham was silent for a moment as he regarded his daughter. 'She obviously cares about you and Beth a great deal. There's something different about her now she's with you. For the first time ever she seems as if she is opening up, unfolding like a flower…and it's obviously down to you. But a word of warning, Steven; tread warily, don't hurt her…or you'll have me to deal with.'

Steven smiled at that.

'You think I'm joking, but I'm not. I already carry a burden of guilt for abandoning Chloe. I've let her down once; I won't do it again.'

Steven turned fully in his chair to look at the other man. 'I think you had better tell me exactly what you are talking about.'

'I'm not going to go into details, Steven. Suffice to say, my first wife left me for a man who seemed a bit of a charmer, a philanderer—I thought he was nothing worse than that. Otherwise I would never have abandoned Chloe to him.'

Steven's eyes narrowed on the older man's face.

'To outward appearances Michael was an upright citizen, a successful lawyer. Who would have believed such a man would be capable of such cruelty?' Graham continued, his voice defensive now. 'My ex-wife was an intelligent and very beautiful woman; I never thought she would subject Chloe to a man like that… But, reading between the lines, it seems Michael ruled the house with a regime of fear—certainly, Chloe was terrified of him; maybe my ex-wife was as well.'

'So, how evil was this Michael?' Steven asked, his tone low and horrified.

'Extremely violent, by all accounts.' Graham looked down at the drink in front of him. 'I didn't know how bad things were, Steven, I swear to you. I'm ashamed to say I was too busy rebuilding my own life here with Margaret. When Chloe came a couple of times on holiday I knew she was a bit withdrawn, but I thought it was because she was missing her mother... I had no idea...' He shook his head. 'Afterwards, when finally she came to live with me, I asked her why she hadn't told me, and she said that if she had told me I'd have made her come to live here, and, although she'd wanted to be with me very much, she'd felt she couldn't leave her mother because she was worried about her, scared for her; she'd felt she needed to be there to look after her.' Graham shook his head sadly. 'She was eleven when she told me that... You've no idea how it made me feel.'

Steven looked over at Chloe and suddenly so many things made sense—the wariness, the way she fought to keep her barriers up, and her tenderness and deep empathy for Beth, especially when Helen had been unsympathetic. Suddenly it all slotted into place and he felt a deep anger at the man who had hurt her so much.

'I'll never know the full extent of what she suffered, but I do know that she had nightmares for a long time afterwards...' Graham fell silent for a while and around them the revelry in the bar suddenly seemed too cheerful. 'I've never talked about this to anyone outside the family before...apart from the people who needed to know, obviously.' Graham finished his drink. 'And I wouldn't have told you except that Chloe is different around you, and maybe it will help you to understand her. She says she's over it now, but sometimes I don't think she is and I worry about her a lot.'

Chloe came over to them at that moment. 'What are you two looking so serious about?' she said.

'Men's talk,' Graham said with a smile as he got up to go to the bar.

Chloe slipped into his seat. 'What was he saying to you?'

she asked lightly. 'He wasn't giving you the third degree, was he? Shining a big light in your eye and asking you what your intentions are?'

Steven laughed. 'He was telling me what a beautiful voice you have.'

'Oh, Dad thinks I do everything well.'

'He might have a point.' Steven smiled. 'Do you want to get out of here?' he asked her suddenly. 'Get some fresh air and walk back to the house?'

She looked into his eyes and saw the seriousness in their dark depths. Her heart started to beat with an uneven rhythm. 'Yes, let's go home,' she said softly.

They walked slowly back along the narrow country lane that hugged the mountainside. There were no street lamps but a full moon shimmered in the sky, bathing the sea below them and the ribbon of road ahead of them in silver.

'Looks like Sinead is going to get a good day for her wedding tomorrow,' Chloe said, breaking the silence.

'Yes, looks like it.'

Chloe glanced sideways at Steven, wondering why he seemed so quiet, so withdrawn. It was as if he was miles away in his thoughts.

Suddenly she remembered that he had probably rung the office this afternoon. She hoped he hadn't received bad news. 'Did you manage to get through to the office while I was out?' she asked, trying to sound nonchalant.

'Yes, I did.'

Chloe stopped walking. 'Is that all you are going to say?' she asked impatiently.

He stopped and looked over at her, and for a moment humour darted over his features. 'What else is there to say?' he asked teasingly.

'Oh, come on, Steven, put me out of my suspense. You know very well what I'm asking. Did Renaldo sign the contract?'

'As a matter of fact, he did,' Steven said with a smile. 'At four-thirty this afternoon Cavendish Enterprises were officially amalgamated with The House of Renaldo, giving us approximately sixty new restaurants on the continent of Europe—'

With a shriek of pleasure Chloe cut across the formality in his tone and flung herself into his arms. 'You did it! I'm so thrilled for you, Steven.'

'Well, I did it with your help,' he said. 'We make a good team, you and I, don't we?'

She looked up at him then, suddenly aware of the fact that they were in each other's arms and that the momentary elation was fading, changing to a very different kind of electricity.

'Yes, I think we do,' she agreed quietly, and felt a thrill of sheer, overwhelming magnitude as he bent his head and kissed her.

She wound her arms tightly around his neck, pressing her body close as she kissed him back with a complete lack of any inhibition. It was no holds barred, a completely intoxicating caress, and she wanted to melt into him, become part of him, and never let him go.

When he released her she was breathless and shaking. 'Wow, that was some kiss.'

He smiled. 'Well, we are celebrating, aren't we?'

She nodded. 'Shall we celebrate some more?' she asked huskily.

He reached and kissed her again, this time so tenderly she felt as if he was reaching into her soul, catching her, holding her. The feeling was unlike anything she had ever known.

She felt almost dizzy when he pulled back and she leaned against him for a moment, loving the feeling of being in his arms. 'I was wrong, Steven, when I said we shouldn't have an affair.' She whispered the words into the darkness.

'I was worried it would affect our working relationship, but I know now that it wouldn't.' She closed her eyes and leaned her head against his chest. 'I mean, we are both adults—we know the score, that it's not serious, and—'

'Chloe,' he broke in.

'Yes.' She pulled back from him and looked up into his eyes dreamily.

'I meant it when I said we made a good team, and I was wondering if you would consider marrying me?'

The question was asked so quietly that for a moment Chloe thought she had misheard him. It was only when she took a step back and really looked into his eyes that she knew she hadn't.

She felt totally and utterly confused.

'That's the question I should have asked you two weeks ago,' Steven continued smoothly. 'I realise now that this is the way forward…move in with me and share my life.'

Chloe felt her heart thumping so heavily it was like a weighted piece of steel in a gym.

'You were right when you said we should keep things businesslike, Chloe. An affair would be wrong for us. Marriage makes much more sense.'

She was so stunned it took a moment before she found her voice. 'Why does marriage make more sense?'

'Because we are such a good team, and you're wonderful with Beth—'

'Are you asking me to marry you because you can't find the right childcare?' She tried to make a joke but her voice was very unsteady.

'I'm asking you because I suddenly realise just what I have in you.' His eyes moved over her seriously. 'And I don't want to lose you.'

'You don't even know me,' she said furiously.

'Of course I know you.' He smiled. 'Chloe, you have

been the most constant woman in my life for the last two years.'

'Have you considered that you might be on the rebound from Helen?' she asked calmly.

For a second Steven stared at her. 'Is that what you think?' He laughed suddenly. 'That's just absurd!'

'No, it's not. Don't you call me absurd.' Chloe glared at him, her eyes dark midnight-blue in the moonlight. 'I won't be used as some kind of substitute childcare! And I resent you even suggesting that I'd consider such a prospect for one moment.'

'What are you talking about?' Steven looked genuinely perplexed. 'I don't need another employee; I'm going to hire one from that bunch you interviewed for me. What I need is a partner...a woman to share my life. The fact that my life includes a six-year-old little girl means that the woman I need has to be very special...I think that woman is you.'

The words took the steam out of her anger. She stared at him. 'And what about love?' The words were a mere whisper in the silence between them.

Steven shrugged. 'You said you didn't believe in it. I'm willing to go with your theory. As you said, marriage should be based on a little more substance than just an illusionary, whimsical feeling...'

Chloe's eyes narrowed on him. 'I don't remember saying that.'

'Oh, you did...not in so many words, but that's the gist of what you were saying to me that night you stayed at my house. You said that this business of the earth moving and lightning zinging through you when you kiss someone is all just a big distraction. That initially a union should be thought out clearly and without emotional trappings, more like a business partnership, so it has some chance of lasting.'

'I'm sure I didn't say all that, Steven, and don't quote me back at myself; it makes me very nervous,' she warned furiously.

He smiled at that. 'Sorry.' He reached across and took hold of her hand. 'So, what do you say?'

'I say you've entirely lost your marbles,' she said drily. Yet the touch of his skin against hers was doing very strange things to her insides.

'I'm a very wealthy man, Chloe. I can look after you—'

'I don't need anyone to look after me,' she interrupted sharply.

'OK, well, maybe I need you more than you need me,' Steven said quietly. 'And in return I could give you everything you want…a nice house, a nice lifestyle… I don't want to lose you at the office, but you'll be free to pursue your career or not; the choice is yours. All I ask is that you are there for Beth when she needs a mother figure.'

'You want me to marry you because Beth needs a mother? Don't you think you need to consider your happiness in all of this?'

'That will make me happy…' he said positively.

She shook her head.

'Don't give me an answer now. Just think about it… We'll go ahead and enjoy the rest of the weekend and you can give me an answer when we return to England.'

When she didn't answer him immediately he reached and put a finger under her chin, tipping her face up firmly so that she was forced to meet his eyes. 'Have we got a deal?'

The touch of his hand against her face made her remember that whispered, husky promise he had made earlier when he had said he wouldn't hurt her.

'You don't have anything to lose by thinking about this, Chloe,' he said softly. 'If you say no there will be no hard feelings.' He stared into her eyes. 'We'll just continue working together as if I've never asked you.'

She looked at him with scepticism for a second. Maybe he could forget about it and go back to the way things had been between them, but she didn't think that would be so easy.

The sound of a car engine made them break apart just as car headlights rounded the corner. The car slowed down and Chloe could see it was Sinead with Mark.

'Hey, you two, do you want a lift home?' Mark called cheerily as he leaned out of the window.

'We certainly do,' Steven called brightly and, catching hold of Chloe's hand, he led her towards the waiting vehicle.

There was another couple in the back seat of Mark's car and Chloe was forced to sit close to Steven. He put an arm around her, drawing her even closer. The scent of his cologne sent prickles of awareness shooting through her. She found herself remembering the way they had made love that evening at her apartment. The wild, outrageously wanton behaviour mocked her as she tried to tell herself that marrying Steven would be a terrible mistake.

CHAPTER ELEVEN

As Mark pulled the car up outside the house other cars pulled in behind him and it suddenly seemed as if half the pub was descending in the sleepy quietness of the night.

Chloe got separated from Steven and caught up in the crowd that was heading straight for the kitchen, where everyone was congregating and munching on Margaret's baking.

'What will you have for a nightcap?' Sinead asked her as she poured a couple of whiskys for the men. Chloe hadn't been drinking alcohol all night and she didn't particularly want to start now.

'I won't, thanks, Sinead.' She glanced around the throng of people, looking for Steven, but couldn't see him anywhere.

'Oh, go on, have a drink—have a glass of wine,' Sinead said earnestly. 'It's my last night of freedom, Chloe.' Even as she was speaking Sinead was pouring the wine.

'I can't believe that I'm going to be a married woman tomorrow,' she said, perching on the arm of a chair. 'It all feels a bit unreal somehow.'

Her own life felt a bit unreal as well, Chloe thought sardonically as across the room she caught sight of Steven talking to Margaret. He looked quite nonchalantly at ease, as if that bizarre proposal had never happened. As she watched she saw an attractive brunette sidling over to him to engage him in conversation. After a little while they were both laughing easily, the woman coquettishly fluttering her eyelashes.

If she married him that was what she would have to put

up with, Chloe thought angrily. She couldn't live a life with him knowing that he didn't love her, that what they had was just a business arrangement for the sake of his daughter. Every woman he spoke to she'd wonder if this was the one he would fall in love with, if this was the one he would leave her for.

She frowned suddenly and reached for her wine.

She had never considered her relationship with Nile as a business arrangement until they had finished, and then suddenly she had wondered if that was all it had been—a convenient arrangement for them both. She had felt safe with Nile and he had drifted along with her. But as soon as it had suited him he'd had no hesitation in finishing with her immediately. Maybe Steven would be the same?

Trouble was, what she felt for Steven was a whole lot different from what she had felt for Nile.

She watched Steven laughing. He had a lovely laugh, warm and inviting. In fact, everything about him was warm and wonderful and… And she was in love with him. The stark truth hit her out of nowhere.

'I'm in love with Steven Cavendish.'

'Sorry, Sis, what did you say?' Sinead looked up from her conversation with one of her old school friends.

'Nothing.' Chloe took another sip of the wine. 'Nothing; don't mind me. All this talk of weddings is mashing my brains.'

Sinead giggled. 'That's what love can do to a woman, Chloe, if she's not very careful.'

Well, not to me, Chloe thought angrily, definitely not to me. She put the glass down. 'I'm going to turn in, Sinead. I'm really tired.'

'Yes, and you should as well, Sinead,' Margaret said as she came over to them. 'You want to be fresh for your big day. Don't forget that you and Chloe have a hairdresser and beauty appointment at nine.'

Sinead pulled a face. 'I'll be fine, Mum; stop fussing.'

Steven looked across the room; he was desperately trying to get away from the woman who was talking to him, and he'd made several polite attempts, but each time she had detained him with a hand on his arm.

'So, who did you say you were here with?' She smiled.

'Sinead's sister Chloe.'

'Oh, right. I'm Mark's sister, by the way, Anita.'

'Pleased to meet you.' Steven saw that Chloe had gone.

'She's gone to bed, Steven,' Margaret said as she passed by and saw him looking around the room.

'Thanks, Margaret. In that case, I'll turn in myself.' He smiled at Anita. 'See you tomorrow.'

'Yes, see you tomorrow.' Anita watched him leave with a flicker of disappointment in her eyes.

As Steven walked down the corridor towards their bedroom he decided to check on Beth before turning in.

The children's room was in darkness, but the door was ajar. He pushed it open a little wider and saw Chloe sitting on the edge of Beth's bed.

'Hi,' he whispered, and came further into the room. The peaceful sound of the children's breathing filled the darkness. Sarah and Jane were top-to-toe in one bed, and Beth was on her own in the other.

He noticed that his daughter had the doll that Chloe had bought her for her birthday tucked in beside her, and next to her on the bedside table was her favourite storybook.

'I wonder how many times Ellie had to read *The Elves and the Shoemaker* tonight?' Steven said, looking down at Beth with an indulgent smile.

'I used to like that story when I was Beth's age,' Chloe said. 'Must be something to do with the idea of going to bed and then when you wake up in the morning all your problems are magically solved.'

The light from the hallway behind him illuminated her as she turned to look up at him.

Steven had always sensed her vulnerability, and he was aware of it now more than ever. He wanted to wrap her up in his arms and protect her, shut out the dark memories, the uncertainty, and just hold her.

'Was that around the time when your mother remarried?' he asked softly.

'How do you know about that?' Her eyes narrowed.

'Just something your dad said.' Steven carefully kept his voice casual. 'He said you had a bad time with your step-father.'

'He was out of order telling you that.' Although Chloe's voice was low, it was filled with anger.

She got up from the bed and made to turn away. But Steven caught hold of her arm. 'Don't run away from me, Chloe,' he said quietly.

She looked down at the hand he had placed on her and he immediately let it drop.

'What else did he tell you?' she asked, her voice unsteady.

Steven hesitated. 'Not a lot... Just that your mother had remarried and you didn't like the guy. I was surprised you hadn't told me about it.'

'There's nothing to tell.' She walked out of the room and back into her own bedroom.

She had left the bedside lamp on and its soft light played over the feminine surroundings, the inviting softness of the double bed. The tranquillity of the scene did nothing to still Chloe's racing heart. She felt furious that her father had mentioned Michael to Steven. He knew that she didn't want to be reminded of that time...how dared he even breathe that man's name?

Chloe paced around the room, and when the door opened

and Steven came in she turned on him angrily. 'Leave me alone.'

'I don't want to leave you alone, Chloe,' he said gently. 'I'm sorry if I've upset you by mentioning your stepfather.'

She shook her head, her eyes over-bright. 'That was the worst time of my life, Steven. I just don't want to be reminded of it.'

'Sometimes in order to let go of the past you have to face up to it, Chloe.'

'I've tried to…'

He came closer to her and she backed away. 'You're not frightened of me, are you?' For a second Steven looked horrified.

'No…no, of course not,' she said emphatically, and watched him visibly relax.

'But you are angry with me?'

'I'm not angry with you, I'm…' She looked into the darkness of his eyes. 'I'm afraid.' She admitted the truth huskily. She was scared—scared of the feelings that Steven could conjure up in her with so little effort. Scared of where all this was leading.

'Afraid of what?' he asked gently.

'Marriage and all it entails.' She shook her head helplessly.

'But you were going to marry Nile.'

She looked up and met his eyes. She wanted to tell him that Nile had never made her feel like this, had never made her lose control of her emotions so completely. 'I don't know if I would have gone through with marrying Nile…' she whispered. 'To be honest, I was having doubts before the break-up.'

His eyes narrowed on her. 'Why?'

'Just frightened of making a mistake. My mother had such a bad relationship… Do you know what it's like to live in a house where there is so much shouting that you have to bury your head under the pillows to stop yourself hearing…?' Chloe's voice trembled for a second. 'They said they were in love, but it destroyed them in the end.'

'All relationships aren't like that, Chloe.'

She tried very hard to gather herself together. 'Maybe not…but I…I just wish you hadn't proposed to me.'

One dark eyebrow rose.

'Don't look at me like that, Steven. You shouldn't have done it. Things were all right the way they were.' Her tone was forceful.

'No, they were not.' Steven smiled.

His cool, composed manner really irritated Chloe. 'Yes, they were. We could have had a nice, uncomplicated affair. And now you've just gone and ruined everything.' She glared up at him angrily.

'I disagree.' He reached out and pulled her closer to him. 'I've just upped the stakes, that's all. I haven't ruined anything.' He tipped her face up so that she was forced to look at him. Then he kissed her. It was such a sweet and tender kiss that it made Chloe's body ache with a desire, a need that was more than just sexual. She loved this man…loved him with all her heart.

'I want to make love to you, Chloe.' He whispered the words against her lips. 'I want you so much, and I want you to know that this isn't just a brief interlude of pleasure; I want more than that. I want us to be a happy family together.'

His gentle words stilled the inner turmoil.

She felt his hands burning through the delicate material of her dress as they rested on her waist.

Tentatively she put her hands onto his shoulders. Then she kissed him back, fiercely, her fear melting as if the desert sun had suddenly come out from behind a cloud.

'I want you too,' she admitted breathlessly as she moved

closer against him, longing to feel his body pressed against hers.

Deftly he slid the zip on her dress down and she didn't try to stop him; instead she kissed him again with impatience and a fever of need.

She wouldn't think about anything, she'd just enjoy what they had, she told herself as she wound herself even closer, and suddenly he swept her up off her feet and carried her towards the deep comfort of the double bed.

Then they were undressing each other with frantic, eager need.

Chloe's dress fell to the ground along with Steven's shirt. She was wearing an oyster satin bra that cupped the fullness of her breasts and a matching pair of briefs. His eyes moved over her slowly and provocatively for a moment. He leant over her and kissed her again on the lips, his hands stroking up over the curves of her waist and then caressing her breast through the satin of her underwear. The sensation was so sweetly tormenting that Chloe longed for him to remove the flimsy barrier. She wound her arms up and around his neck and kissed him hungrily, her lips parting in complete surrender as his tongue played provocatively with her.

Then her hands trailed over the strong, powerful muscles of his torso and came to rest on the waistband of his trousers.

He pulled away from her and removed the rest of his clothing.

She sat up slightly to watch him. He had the most magnificent, powerful body; she moved her eyes over him, noting the width of his shoulders, the muscles on his arms, the narrowness of his hips and the curve of his buttocks. He turned, caught her watching him, and smiled as she blushed.

He stood next to the bed, staring down at her, his eyes dark and intense.

Then he straddled her and reached to unfasten her bra. Slowly he bent to kiss her breasts, his breath soft and tickling against the sensitised skin.

Gently he kissed her neck, her shoulders, his mouth travelling down over her, kissing every part of her with a thoroughness that made her catch her breath, made her body cry out with the need to feel him inside.

But his movements were leisurely and tender; gently he pulled her panties down, his lips following where his fingers played until she gasped with pleasure.

Gently and with exquisite care he took her to new heights of ecstasy so that she writhed uncontrollably in his arms.

'Beautiful Chloe.' He whispered the words as he entered her. 'Beautiful, delectable, wonderful Chloe.'

When Chloe woke sunshine was flooding over the room; she smiled and stretched lazily. Then she opened her eyes and found Steven lying next to her. He was propped up on one elbow, watching her.

'Good morning, beautiful,' he smiled.

She smiled back at him sleepily. 'How long have you been watching me?'

'Not long enough.' His eyes drifted lower and she realised suddenly that she was completely naked—not even the sheets covered her. She reached out instinctively to pull the covers up, but he stopped her.

'It's a bit late for modesty where I'm concerned,' he growled, rolling over to pin her to the bed and kiss her hungrily and thoroughly on the lips. 'I really enjoyed last night,' he murmured.

'So did I,' she admitted.

'Yes, I noticed.' He smiled as she blushed. 'I love the

way I can make you blush,' he said huskily. 'Like a virgin on her wedding night.'

'Don't be silly.' She smiled and tried to escape him as he tried to kiss her again. But he wouldn't allow her to move, his mouth teasing her provocatively, causing her to heat up inside with instant desire.

'Do you know what I'd like to do when we get home?' he asked suddenly.

'No.' She looked up at him warily.

'I'd like to make love to you in the office, take you over my desk, kiss you senseless in the middle of the afternoon, ruffle those neat business suits of yours.'

'Now you really are being silly,' she said breathlessly.

'Why?'

'Well… You know that the middle of the afternoon is our busiest time.' She smiled up at him teasingly. 'Late afternoon would be much better.'

He laughed. 'Did I ever tell you that you are the perfect PA?' He punctuated the words with kisses.

'I think you might have mentioned something.'

'But before I make love to you in the office you are going to have to agree to marry me.' He whispered the words against her ear. 'I'll have to make an honest woman out of you before taking such liberties.'

He felt her stiffen underneath him, felt her mood change. 'Don't talk marriage, Steven,' she pleaded huskily.

'It's not an immoral suggestion, sweetheart.' He found her lips and kissed her again. She kissed him back, but hesitantly now.

The sound of children laughing came from the hallway. Steven raised his head and listened for a moment, then regretfully pulled away from her. 'I'd better go and see to Beth,' he murmured.

'Yes…' She let her breath out in a sigh of relief.

'Hey.' He bent and gave her one last very firm, very sensual kiss. 'But we'll continue this discussion later.'

As he got up from the bed Chloe reached for her dressing gown. 'I've got a hairdresser's appointment at nine,' she said. 'And a wedding to go to; let's stick to your original plan and discuss all that when we get home.'

Steven made no reply.

The peppery scent of freesias spiced the air in the cool darkness of the church as Sinead and Mark took their vows.

Chloe had never seen her sister more beautiful, more radiant than she was today. As Mark slipped the ring onto her finger and the priest pronounced them man and wife Sinead looked into her husband's eyes and smiled, with a trusting, loving look that tore at Chloe's heart.

Next to her, Sarah and Jane started to fidget with their flowers, the stiffened silk of their long blue dresses rustling in the silence. Chloe slanted a look at them and they stopped immediately and smiled at her, looking like two angels with their haloes of flowers on their dark curls.

Chloe smiled back, amused by their look of innocence. Then as she looked up she met Steven's eyes in the congregation. His smile, a tender, indulgent look, did very strange things to her heart. Quickly she looked away, back towards the altar.

'Give them the power to make a home where love and peace and honour shall abide.' Chloe closed her eyes, the priest's voice resounding through her.

A warm breeze caught the confetti and it swirled through the air in a wild mosaic against the blue sky, landing on everyone.

Steven watched Chloe as she tried to brush it away from the blue silk dress. She looked stunning: the elegant dress skimmed her figure, leaving her shoulders bare, showing the long, creamy perfection of her neck. Her hair was wound up on top of her head and threaded through with tiny white flowers. As he watched she turned her head and caught his eye. Then she smiled and walked across towards him.

'I think they've almost finished taking the photographs now,' she said.

'You look beautiful, Chloe,' he said, and then leaned closer to whisper against her ear. 'I want you all to myself—when can we escape from all these people?'

'Let's see.' She pretended to count the hours. 'Well, we've got the meal and then the speeches and then the party…say, about eleven or twelve hours, give or take an hour.'

Steven groaned. 'I don't think I'm going to contain myself for that long.'

Beth ran over towards them, panting with excitement. She looked very cute in a white dress with sprigs of pink roses embossed on the fabric, her long curls caught back from her face with slides. 'Daddy, can I ride to the hotel in the car with Jane and Sarah?' Her face was flushed from running as she looked from Steven to Chloe. 'Please… please?'

'I don't think so, Beth,' Steven said. 'Sarah and Jane are going in the official limousine with Chloe and Margaret.'

Beth's face fell. 'Wish I had been a flower girl,' she said.

'Never mind, Beth.' Chloe stepped in to the rescue. 'I think it might be all right for you to go in the car with Sarah and Jane, now that the ceremony is over. You can take my place and I'll go in the car with Daddy.' Flicking an inquisitive look up at Steven, she smiled. 'I think that might just solve two problems today, don't you?'

Steven smiled back at her. 'If Margaret wouldn't mind, that would be great.'

'I don't think it will be a problem.' Chloe held out her

hand to the little girl. 'Come on, let's go check and see what Margaret has to say.'

Steven watched his daughter skipping across the grass happily next to Chloe, his smile still on his face. He hoped the ride to the hotel was a very long one.

The narrow lane was lined with lime trees that overhung, giving the effect of driving up through a green tunnel. 'Are you sure we can drive along here?' Steven asked Chloe with a grin.

'Trust me, there's a great view from up here.'

Steven shook his head. 'I've got all the view I want right here in this car.' Teasingly he added, 'Why don't we just stop the car here?'

'Just keep driving,' she said firmly. 'We haven't got that long anyway. I reckon they'll have a few drinks outside on the lawn before they go into the hotel for the meal, so we've got about half an hour.'

The lane widened and suddenly in front of them Steven could see a dazzling view down over the sea.

Below them lay a sheltered cove with powdery white sand. It was totally deserted and looked like a private beach that went with the one and only house up on the headland— a white mansion that was built on two levels into the cliff face.

'That's some view,' Steven said.

'I used to come here sometimes with Dad and Margaret on picnics when I came to stay with Dad in the holidays. That was before Sinead was born.'

Steven looked over at her. He wanted to ask her about those days, but there was a faraway expression in her blue eyes, and he didn't want to upset her.

'I used to wonder who lived in that house.' She nodded towards the cliff. 'It's called Perfect Haven.' Chloe smiled. 'Can you imagine living in the perfect haven?'

'If the right person is with you I'm sure anywhere can be the perfect haven.'

Chloe transferred her attention to Steven. 'You say the loveliest things sometimes.'

'That's because you inspire me.' He smiled the crooked smile that was so teasing and charming. Then he leaned across towards her and kissed her softly. 'We can make our own perfect haven once you say yes to me.'

'You promised me that we wouldn't talk about that,' she whispered.

'Did I?' He frowned. 'In that case, I'll settle for some passionate kissing instead.'

As he leaned even closer she laughed breathlessly. 'Don't smudge my make-up too much, Stevie…'

'OK, here's the deal. You agree to marry me and I don't smudge your make-up…too much.' He looked at her with warmth in his eyes.

'That's not a fair deal. Anyway, we already made a deal and that was that I think about your proposal and give you my answer when we get home.'

'Those were last night's terms,' Steven said, shaking his head. 'And, as you didn't agree with them at the time, we're going to have to renegotiate them.'

'Excuse me! That mumbo-jumbo stuff might have worked with Renaldo, but it won't wash with me,' she said, a spark of humour in her voice.

'Is that so?' Steven grinned. 'Right, well, you asked for it—I'm just going to have to mercilessly smudge your make-up. And everyone back at the wedding reception will know very well what you've been up to on the drive to the hotel.'

She reached for the door handle. 'You'll have to catch me first,' she said with a laugh.

Kicking off her shoes as soon as she stepped out of the car, she ran down the path towards the beach, holding her dress well up out of the way as she jumped the last few inches down onto the sand.

Steven ran after her, and she laughed when he made a dive for her and missed as she dodged him successfully and ran further along the beach.

It was really no contest and he easily caught her a few minutes later, swinging her around, her dress swirling in the breeze. She laughed as he held her firmly around her waist and reached down to kiss her.

'OK, I give in,' she said, winding her arms up around his neck. 'Guess I'll have to go back to the reception with smudged make-up.'

'That's not all you'll have to go back to the wedding with.' Before she realised his intention he swung her up into his arms, carrying her down towards the water's edge.

'Steven!' Her eyes widened in horror. 'Now, come on, a joke's a joke but this is going too far.' She looked up at him, a bit disconcerted when she saw the determined expression on his handsome face.

'Now, what's it to be?' he said as he swung her precariously over the waves that lapped in over his dark polished shoes.

She tightened her arms around his neck. 'Steven, stop!'

'Imagine all those faces at that wedding reception when you walk in wet through.' He smiled into her eyes and she really couldn't work out any more if he was joking or not.

'Steven, this isn't fair...'

He bent his head and kissed her. It was such a passionate kiss that she was completely breathless when he raised his head. 'So, what's it to be?' he asked gently. 'Will you do me the honour of becoming Mrs Cavendish...?'

She smiled and, reaching up, kissed him again, the sound of the waves washing around them filling her senses. Happiness bubbled inside her; suddenly this felt so right... 'How can I possibly refuse?' she whispered.

CHAPTER TWELVE

SIX weeks after their return from Ireland Chloe still felt as
if she was on some magical merry-go-round.

A huge diamond ring sparkled on her finger; Steven was
attentive, gentle...loving. Her mind skipped over the last
word. All right, he hadn't said he loved her—in fact, quite
the opposite if she replayed his actual proposal in her mind.
But when she thought about Steven proposing she preferred
to think about those few minutes on the beach when he had
swept her off her feet and whirled her around, kissing her
with such passion... That was the real proposal she wanted
to remember.

They were going out to dinner tonight to discuss wedding arrangements. And this weekend Chloe was going to
stay at Steven's house and they were going to tell Beth.

Chloe's heart skipped every time she thought about it.
Once they told Beth there would be no going back; she had
said as much to Steven, asking that they had a few weeks'
grace before telling the little girl.

It wasn't that Chloe wanted to back out, just that she
wanted a bit of time to get used to the idea before it all
became public knowledge. She had thought Steven might
argue the point, but he had agreed. With that in mind they
had only got the ring yesterday. Every time it caught the
office lights she got a thrill of delight.

The phone rang on her desk and Chloe picked it up,
forcing herself to concentrate on work. 'Steven Cavendish's
personal assistant speaking.'

'Hi, Chloe, it's Helen.'

The familiar voice brought a wave of disturbance rushing into Chloe's well-ordered world.

'I believe congratulations are in order—Steven tells me you are getting married.'

'Yes, that's right.' Chloe wondered when Steven had seen Helen to impart that information. He hadn't mentioned the meeting to her.

'I wish you all the best with the arrangement,' Helen said briskly. 'You're so good with Beth; just what Steven wanted. Put me through to him, will you, Chloe?'

Chloe would have liked to disconnect her, but she forced herself to remain businesslike. 'Hold on a minute, please; I'll just see if he's in the office.'

She knew full well that Steven was in his office, but she was unsure if he would take the call or not. She flicked the button on the intercom. 'Steven, Helen Smyth-Jones is on the phone for you,' she said, hoping her voice held its usual professional tone.

There was a moment's silence. 'OK, put her through,' Steven said.

Chloe flicked the switch and did as he asked. Then she sat and looked at the phone as if it had suddenly turned into some kind of serpent. What did Helen want? And why hadn't Steven told her that he'd seen her? The urge to turn a switch and listen in to their conversation was very strong. But she forced herself to turn her attention back to her computer.

But if concentrating on work had been difficult before it seemed impossible now. *I wish you all the best with the arrangement.* Helen's words played jeeringly over in her mind. That was a strange thing to have said, a strange choice of words. It was almost as if Helen knew that Steven didn't love her, knew the terms of his proposal. But how could she? Unless Steven had told her?

Chloe glanced again at the phone. The light was still on;

they were still talking. It was a long conversation for a man to have with an ex-girlfriend, she thought warily, especially a man who was engaged to someone else.

At last the light went off and Chloe tried to relax.

She felt her skin start to prickle and itch again, something it had been doing for over a week now. It was driving her crazy. She had joked with Steven last week when he had caught her rubbing at her arms that she must be allergic to him. He hadn't looked very amused. She smiled now as she remembered that conversation and glanced at her watch. She had made an appointment with the doctor for five-thirty. Hurriedly she finished off typing the rest of the letters, because it was almost time for her to leave.

The door from Steven's office opened and he came out. 'Do you have those figures from Paris?' he asked distractedly.

'Yes.' She searched through the pile of papers next to her and handed him the relevant one.

'Fine…thanks.' He ran an eye down the page. 'Great.' He smiled at her and seemed to be about to just return to his office without saying anything else.

'Steven?' She stopped him before he could turn away.

'Yeah?'

'What did Helen want?'

'Oh, that! She's bringing a party of clients to the Waterside next week and she wanted to know if I'd have a word with Jamie, make sure they got the red-carpet treatment…as if I haven't got enough to do.' He shook his head impatiently. 'I told her I'd look into it for her, but why the hell she just couldn't have rung Jamie and sorted it out herself is beyond me.'

She should have known it was just something like that; Chloe smiled. 'I just wondered,' she said with a shrug.

He frowned as he noticed her rubbing her skin. 'Are you still bothered with that prickly heat?'

'I told you, I'm allergic to you.'

'Nonsense, you're just too hot to handle, that's what it is.' Steven smiled. 'There's molten lava going through your veins. I knew it the first time I kissed you.'

He watched her flush and smiled. 'But, on a more serious note, maybe you should go and see about it? Could be something that Beth has unwittingly passed on to you— chicken pox, for instance?'

'I've already had that and, anyway, if that was the case Beth would have it as well. 'I'm going to pop into Dr Hallowell on the way home, get some cream; it could be a reaction to washing powder or something.'

Steven nodded. 'Oh, by the way, I'm going to have to go to Paris on Friday to look over one of the new restaurants; I'll be back Saturday afternoon. You couldn't hold the fort here and with Beth, could you? That new nanny tells me she can't cover Friday night or Saturday—she's got some family reunion booked.'

'That's OK, I'll see to everything,' Chloe said easily.

'Thanks, Chloe. Pack a few things in your overnight bag; maybe you could stay a bit longer than one night. And, of course, you will pack something special to wear for when I take you and Beth out for lunch when we return from Paris.'

'Sorry? What did you say?' She looked up at him with a frown.

'I said when I return from Paris I shall take you and Beth out for lunch,' he said impatiently. 'You hadn't forgotten that we are telling Beth our news this weekend?'

'No, of course not. It's just…you said when *we* return from Paris.'

'Did I?' Steven shrugged. 'Well, I meant when *I* return…sorry.'

Chloe noticed the slight hesitation in meeting her eyes as he corrected himself, and she felt a sick thud of her heart.

She had the most awful feeling that he was hiding something.

As Steven turned back into his office he wondered if he had got away with that slip of the tongue just now.

As she waited for Dr Hallowell Chloe pretended to be interested in the glossy magazines sitting next to her. But in reality her mind was buzzing back over the conversation that had just taken place between herself and Steven.

Was it a coincidence that Steven had suddenly decided to go to Paris for the night just after speaking to Helen on the phone? The question tormented her, as did that slip he had made. 'After *we* return from Paris.'

Chloe flicked through the magazine. It was just a simple slip-up, just one word of a mistake; it meant nothing, and she told herself so, over and over. Yet there was something about the way he hadn't been able to meet her eyes that made the sentence continually torment her.

The receptionist called her name, jogging her out of her contemplation, and it was almost a feeling of relief to go into the doctor's surgery and take her mind off the problem.

A little while later, however, she was facing a different dilemma.

CHAPTER THIRTEEN

PREGNANT: the word screamed through Chloe's subconscious as she sat in her apartment in a state of semi-shock. All right, she was a little bit late, but that wasn't unusual for her. She had never suspected... It was just an annoying little itch; how could that mean she was pregnant?

Hormonal reaction, the doctor had said, his voice matter-of-fact. After questioning her he had estimated that she was probably two months pregnant. Which must mean it had happened that evening at her apartment when Steven had walked her home.

Chloe glanced at the clock beside her. Steven was due to pick her up in about an hour. She didn't want to see him, couldn't face him until she had decided on what to say to him...

They had never discussed having children of their own. She knew he had wanted a big family with his wife, but he had loved her. Suddenly those little missing words were like a huge hole inside her. All these weeks since coming back from Ireland she had been living in a dream world, telling herself that Steven would grow to love her one day...but what if that wasn't the case? It was one thing taking the risk and marrying him without love when it was just her...but a baby...a baby made the situation suddenly seem glaringly precarious.

She needed to sleep on this and face Steven in the morning, she decided abruptly. There was no way she could have dinner with him, not now, with this knowledge burning away inside her.

As she reached for the phone Chloe glanced at her watch.

It was too late to cancel. Steven would already have left, and, even if she caught him on his mobile, knowing Steven, he would still arrive.

She'd have to get ready and face the evening as best she could. Hurriedly she went through to her bedroom to shower and change.

Chloe chose a lilac-coloured trouser suit from her wardrobe and left her hair loose. She studied her reflection critically in the mirror.

The strange thing was that she did look good—glowing, in fact. And as well as that she had actually lost weight! How was that possible, she wondered.

Maybe the doctor had made a mistake?

Steven was ten minutes early. He bounded up the stairs, looking refreshed and relaxed in a pale grey suit that did incredible things for an already perfect physique.

He smiled at her. 'How did you get on with Dr Hallowell?'

The quietly asked question made her temperature soar.

'Fine.' Her smile was slightly strained. 'Pretty much as we suspected... I'm allergic to you. The doctor said to break off all contact immediately, or it could be fatal.'

'I demand a second opinion at a Harley Street specialist.' Steven grinned. 'Because you won't get out of marrying me that easily.'

She picked up her bag and swiftly changed the subject. 'I'm ready to go if you are.'

As usual the Waterside Restaurant was busy, but they were escorted immediately to their table.

As Chloe studied the menu she couldn't help remembering the last time they had come here, on her birthday. Never in her wildest dreams had she thought she would be in here just over six weeks later with an engagement ring on her finger and the knowledge that she was pregnant.

The waiter brought some champagne and as he poured it Chloe suddenly realised that if she was pregnant she shouldn't drink. 'May I have a bottle of mineral water, please?' she asked the waiter before he departed.

She smiled across at him. 'How's Beth getting on with the new nanny?'

'Fine... Beth really likes Paula. She was a good choice, Chloe.'

Chloe nodded. She had been the last of the women on her interview list. And Chloe had liked her instantly.

'So...' Steven settled back in his chair and raised his glass. 'Shall we drink to a June wedding?'

Chloe looked at him in consternation. 'We're midway through June now!'

'Well, we'll have to settle on a date.' Although his voice was light-hearted there was something about the way he was watching her that was very intense. 'And there's no point in hanging around.'

Silently she agreed that they should settle on a date, and under the circumstances it probably should be sooner rather than later. But she couldn't go ahead and blithely make plans until she had told him her news, and she wasn't ready for that tonight.

The waiter came and took their order. When he had gone again Chloe hoped to change the subject but Steven persisted. 'So, what about a July wedding, then?'

'July...' She felt hot and uncomfortable.

'Are you happy about having a registry-office service? If you'd rather we can book a church,' Steven said.

'No. I don't want a whole big fuss. Just a quiet civil ceremony.'

'Well, at least you haven't changed your mind.'

The quietly spoken words made her glance over at him. He was watching her with a raised eyebrow. 'You had me a bit worried for a moment.'

The waiter approached the table and said something to Steven quietly. Something that Chloe couldn't hear.

Steven shook his head. 'Sorry, Chloe, Jamie wants a quiet word with me in the office. Will you excuse me for a moment?'

'Yes...sure.' She took a sip of her water and watched him crossing the crowded restaurant with a determined stride.

So, what to do? The question burned inside her. Should she tell him now and see what he said?

The ring of Steven's mobile phone, which was lying on the table, interrupted her thoughts. Chloe reached and picked it up, seeing Helen's name flashing on the screen.

She hesitated, then clicked the connect button.

'Hello, darling, just wanted a quick word about Paris...' Helen purred. Chloe reacted immediately by disconnecting her and sat back, stunned.

Suddenly Steven's earlier slip of the tongue became clear. He was taking Helen to Paris. She felt cold inside.

'Have I had a phone call?' Steven's voice made her jump. She looked up at him, her eyes wide, and realised she was still clutching his phone.

'Yes.' She swallowed on a lump in her throat.

'Who was it?' he asked, taking his seat opposite.

'I don't know...' she lied, handing him back his phone.

It rang again. Chloe knew very well that it would be Helen's name flashing on that screen as the woman tried to call him back. She waited for him to answer it, but instead he switched it off and put it back down on the table.

'I'm sure, whatever it is, it's not important,' he said quietly. 'They can leave a message on the answering service.' Then he noted the pallor of her skin.

'Are you all right?' he asked with concern.

Chloe couldn't gather herself together to answer him.

'Chloe?'

She was aware that Steven was talking, but his voice seemed to be coming from a long way away. 'Do you think we could get out of here?' she asked. 'I don't feel very well.'

'Yes, of course.' Steven frowned and immediately put up his hand and summoned the waiter.

Chloe was feeling incredibly claustrophobic, as if the whole restaurant was suddenly closing in on her. She was aware that Jamie had arrived at the table now, asking Steven if everything was all right.

'Yes, everything is fine. We just have to leave...' Steven's voice was firm and polite. But the manager still detained him.

Without waiting around, Chloe headed downstairs and left the restaurant.

The air outside was cool and misty with rain. It was dark now and the rain was illuminated like a silver sheet against the glare of the street lamps.

She walked over towards the embankment and stared out at the darkness of the river.

Why did this hurt so much? she wondered. Why did she have this searing pain wedged somewhere deep inside? She had always known that Steven didn't love her. In fact, he had been quite honest about his intentions. His proposal of marriage had been a business plan... Even right back on that night when they had made love he had talked about their union in businesslike terms; how was it he had phrased it...the perfect arrangement...?

She was aware of Steven coming out of the restaurant behind her. 'Chloe, you're going to get soaked.' He came over to stand beside her. 'Here, take my coat,' he said, draping it around her shoulders. 'What's the matter, sweetheart?'

The endearment was the last straw.

'I can't marry you, Steven.' Her voice was cool and clear

and suddenly wonderfully controlled. 'I'm sorry…I just can't. I've changed my mind.'

Steven shook his head. 'No, you haven't.' His voice was equally firm. 'You're just a bit nervous, that's all—'

'Steven, I mean it.' She tried to take her ring off so that she could give it back to him.

He put out a hand and caught hold of hers, stopping her with gentle force.

'Come back to the car and we'll talk,' he said softly.

She shook her head. 'There's nothing to say.'

'Yes, there is.' Steven held her hand tightly. 'Don't walk away, Chloe.' His voice was low and earnest. 'There's too much at stake here. Think of what you are doing. I need you, Chloe, and Beth needs you—'

'I'm sorry…' Her voice started to break. 'I really am…but at least we haven't told Beth.'

She tried to take her hand away from him, but still he wouldn't let go.

'Why are you doing this?' He spoke quietly, but his eyes blazed into hers.

'That phone call a moment ago was from Helen; she wanted to talk to you about Paris.' She blurted out the words, unable to contain them any longer.

Steven frowned. 'Why would Helen want to talk to me about Paris?'

'You tell me.' She looked at him pointedly. 'Come on, Steven, I'm not stupid; you're taking her to Paris, aren't you?'

'No, I am not.' He looked startled. 'I'm amazed you would think that.'

'Really? What was it you said this morning…? ''When I take you and Beth out for lunch when *we* return from Paris.'' And now she's ringing you to talk about the trip. She said, ''Hello, darling, a quick word about Paris.'''

'Well, I don't care what she said—'

'You are still in love with her.' Chloe cut across him. 'I know you are…you even sent her red roses after your relationship had supposedly finished.'

'Roses?' Steven looked perplexed.

'The ones I ordered for you, the ones that were delivered to your house,' she reminded him tersely.

'Oh, those! They weren't for Helen! It was my sister Maddi's wedding anniversary and she and her husband were coming to stay for a few days; the roses were for their anniversary.'

'Oh…' Chloe's anger died a little and she felt a bit foolish for mentioning the flowers now. 'But the fact remains that you are still seeing Helen,' she continued in a lower tone. 'Don't lie to me, Steven. I know the truth—I heard her on the phone.'

Steven got out his mobile phone. 'I don't know what she wanted, but we will sort this out here and now.' Swiftly he pressed the keys and waited.

'Hi, Helen, it's Steven. I believe you phoned me a few moments ago; what's your problem?' His voice was curt. 'I see…' He shook his head. 'Would you mind repeating that?' Swiftly he held the phone to Chloe's ear.

'When you told me this morning you were going to Paris I wondered if you would pick me up some of my favourite perfume; it's not available here now and—'

Steven took the phone back and cut the communication, putting the phone back into his trouser pocket.

'And, before you ask, I've forgotten what Helen's favourite perfume is,' he said briskly. 'How could you think I'd do something as deceitful as see Helen behind your back?'

'I'm sorry, Steven, it was wrong of me.' Her voice was very low. 'I know that. You are an honourable man, Steven Cavendish, a man who adores his daughter—'

'And adores his fiancée,' Steven finished huskily. 'I

would never hurt you like that, Chloe. I couldn't bear to lose you... I love you.'

The words cut into Chloe's consciousness and brought her to an abrupt halt.

'You love me?' Her eyes were wide and incredulous.

'Of course I love you.'

His eyes moved tenderly over her face.

'Oh, Steven!' She went into his arms. 'I love you too.' Her voice was muffled against his chest. Firmly he held her away from him.

'Say that again,' he demanded.

'I said, I love you, Steven Cavendish...'

Steven wrapped her in a bear hug of such proportions that he almost squeezed the breath out of her as he whirled her around.

Then suddenly they were kissing, frantically holding each other, oblivious of the rain and the people going in and out of the restaurant behind him.

It was only when Steven pulled back that they suddenly became aware of how saturated they were. 'I think we should get out of this rain before we catch pneumonia,' Steven said, putting his arm protectively around her, and they hurried to the car.

Once they were in the shelter of the car, he turned to her with a smile. 'Now, where were we?'

'You were telling me how much you love me,' she whispered. 'And I still can hardly believe it.'

'I thought you didn't believe in love?' Steven said teasingly.

'I've had a conversion,' she laughed.

He smiled and traced the outline of her lips with his finger. 'And to think I was so worried about mentioning the dreaded L-word that I went to all those elaborate lengths to avoid it when I proposed...'

'You loved me the day you proposed? I thought it was

just a business proposition…a perfect arrangement of expediency?'

Steven shook his head. 'I was just frightened that if I told you how I felt that it would scare you away…and I wanted you so much I'd have said anything that day to hold you, to keep you in my life…be with you… You've no idea the passions you arouse in me.'

She laughed a little at that. 'I think I have a little idea,' she whispered, remembering the passion of his lovemaking. 'But I thought it was just sexual, and today I was suddenly convinced that you were seeing Helen again.'

'I never loved Helen, Chloe. Never felt about her the way I feel about you.' Steven reached and kissed her tenderly on the lips. 'But your instincts were right about that trip to Paris.' He pulled away from her and opened the dashboard, taking out an envelope.

'What's that?' Chloe asked as he handed it across to her. 'Those are our flight tickets and details. I'm taking *you* with me to Paris, Chloe…as a surprise. Remind me never to try and hoodwink you again.'

Chloe threw her arms around him and hugged him tight. 'Oh, Steven, I love you so much.'

They kissed again and it was a while before they drew apart.

'I've got a surprise as well,' she said quietly, almost shyly, as he looked down at her.

'What kind of surprise?' he asked indulgently.

'Well…firstly…you know you mentioned something about a June wedding?'

'Yes…?'

'Well, maybe that was a good idea…'

As he made to reach to kiss her she pulled away. 'That's not the surprise,' she said quietly.

'It's not?'

She shook her head. 'I was hesitating about setting the

date for our wedding because I have something important to tell you.' She took a deep breath. 'I'm almost two months pregnant, Steven... I found out today—'

For a second Steven looked stunned, then a smile of incredible happiness spread over his face. 'Oh, darling, that's wonderful.'

'So you don't think Beth will mind having a little brother or sister?' she asked.

'Mind?' He laughed. 'She's going to be ecstatic, just like me.'

As Steven pulled her towards him and kissed her with tenderness and love she closed her eyes. 'I think I've found that perfect haven after all,' she whispered happily.

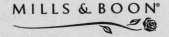

MILLS & BOON

heat *of the* night

LORI FOSTER
GINA WILKINS
VICKI LEWIS THOMPSON

3 SIZZLING SUMMER NOVELS IN ONE

On sale 17th May 2002

Available at most branches of WH Smith,
Tesco, Martins, Borders, Eason, Sainsbury's
and most good paperback bookshops.

FREE
2 BOOKS
AND A SURPRISE GIFT!

We would like to take this opportunity to thank you for reading this Mills & Boon® book by offering you the chance to take TWO more specially selected titles from the Modern Romance™ series absolutely FREE! We're also making this offer to introduce you to the benefits of the Reader Service™—

- ★ FREE home delivery
- ★ FREE monthly Newsletter
- ★ FREE gifts and competitions
- ★ Exclusive Reader Service discount
- ★ Books available before they're in the shops

Accepting these FREE books and gift places you under no obligation to buy; you may cancel at any time, even after receiving your free shipment. Simply complete your details below and return the entire page to the address below. *You don't even need a stamp!*

YES! Please send me 2 free Modern Romance™ books and a surprise gift. I understand that unless you hear from me, I will receive 4 superb new titles every month for just £2.55 each, postage and packing free. I am under no obligation to purchase any books and may cancel my subscription at any time. The free books and gift will be mine to keep in any case.

P2ZEC

Ms/Mrs/Miss/Mr ....Initials ....
BLOCK CAPITALS PLEASE

Surname ....

Address ....

....

....Postcode ....

Send this whole page to:
UK: FREEPOST CN81, Croydon, CR9 3WZ
EIRE: PO Box 4546, Kilcock, County Kildare (stamp required)

Offer valid in UK and Eire only and not available to current Reader Service subscribers to this series. We reserve the right to refuse an application and applicants must be aged 18 years or over. Only one application per household. Terms and prices subject to change without notice. Offer expires 30th September 2002. As a result of this application, you may receive offers from other carefully selected companies. If you would prefer not to share in this opportunity please write to The Data Manager at the address above.

Mills & Boon® is a registered trademark owned by Harlequin Mills & Boon Limited.
Modern Romance™ is being used as a trademark.